To Kaylee Grace and William Emmet,
who, whether they like it or not, were
both born into families of MTNs.

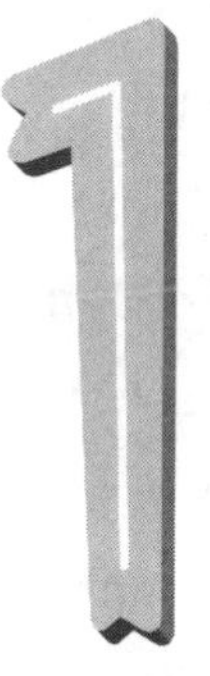

1

Jack

JUST BREATHE, I TOLD MYSELF as my castmates zipped around me, taking last swigs of water or popping a Ricola before making their next entrance. *You've done this a million times before.*

Once again, I'd found myself waiting in the dark, preparing to step onstage and back into the spotlight. I mouthed the lyrics to my song, reciting them under my breath. Even though I was no stranger to the thrills of an opening night, this particular evening felt different.

The action behind the curtain, however, was the same no matter what stage I was on. Dancers stretched out their hamstrings, getting ready for the kick line in the big production number. Dressers raced to their next "quick change," carrying laundry baskets piled high with colorful costumes. Stagehands set out props as vocal warm-ups rang from every dressing room and stage managers shouted commands into their headsets—*"Light cue 23 . . . and go!"*

I wasn't at my middle school, a place where just a few months ago I'd played the lead in a production of *Guys and Dolls*. I wasn't at the local theater in my hometown of Shaker Heights, Ohio. I wasn't even on a Broadway stage.

No, I was in a place that seemed to feel somehow more exotic—a fantasyland nestled in Michigan, a utopia where pianos were as common as lawn mowers and you were more likely to be sore from a dance class than a sunburn, a place where being able to hit a high C and knowing all the lyrics off the *Hamilton* cast album just meant you were one of the cool kids. A place my best friend, Lou (or Louisa Benning, as she was known on her camp forms), had spent hours describing in detail—from the acoustics of the practice rooms to the pine smell of the cubbies where you stored your dance shoes. I was, of course, at Camp Curtain Up.

Lou had been dropping hints about Camp Curtain Up (or CCU, as she liked to call it) from the moment the curtain fell on *Guys and Dolls* this past spring.

"I heard Sebastian and Tanner are both going to soccer camp," she said one day at lunch. "And now that I'm an eighth-grader, I'm going to be gone for *two weeks*. I bet it's going to be *preeetty* empty here in the summer."

Another day I found a pamphlet for the camp tucked beneath the windshield wiper of our family minivan. *Gee, I wonder how that got there?*

Underestimating Lou Benning would have been a mistake. I'd known her tactics from last fall when she tried to convince me to audition for *Into the Woods*. So until my driveway was covered in comedy and tragedy masks drawn with sidewalk chalk, I knew we still had a ways to go.

"You know, I heard on the radio that the Reptile Expo is going up at the I-X Center the same week that I leave for CCU," she said, standing in my kitchen one day, holding one of my mom's homemade fruit pops. "At least you'll have *something* to do while I'm gone. I know how much you love a Gila monster—"

"Lou, before you throw a parade," I cut her off, "you should know, I talked to my mom last night."

"Oh yeah?" she asked meekly, a stream of pink juice dripping down her wrist. "And what did she say?"

Of course I asked my parents if I could go to a place that Lou referred to as "the Hogwarts of Musical Theater." The only reason I hadn't mentioned it to them sooner was that I'd never actually been to a sleepaway camp—a fact to Midwesterners that seemed as strange as saying you'd never tried corn on the cob or gooey butter cake.

"My mom said, 'Sure.'"

If I wasn't holding a sticky juice pop, I was fairly sure my best friend would have leaped into my arms right then and there.

It was such a relief to have Lou joining me at CCU, but the second my mom eased our minivan up to the camp's Broadway marquee–inspired Welcome sign, we were forced to split up.

"Jack, it says here that you're in cabin three,"

my mom said, flipping through the welcome packet. "Oh, and it looks like boys' and girls' cabins are on opposite sides of the camp."

Uh-oh, I thought. *Guess our two-man show could be getting some new costars.*

Enter Teddy Waverly!

The wheels of our car had barely crunched to a halt before I was dashing out the door to the cabin marked with a big wooden "3." Inside were six metal bunk beds, each stacked with a mattress, many with sleeping bags already rolled across them. The only other person in the room was a dark-haired boy, busy unpacking his stuff onto a lower bunk. He was taller than me and wore a white polo shirt tucked into a pair of crisply ironed navy blue pants. Above his loafers, his pant legs were rolled up, revealing an inch of tan, sockless ankle, and his hair was shiny and sharply parted, like he might be carrying a comb in his pocket.

"The top bunk is free," he said, giving me a crooked smile. "I'd take it, but I had a fall at my last camp and busted my lip on the way down. I figured I shouldn't chance it."

"Oh." I gulped. "Yeah, that's probably smart," I said, slinging my backpack to the bunk above him.

This probably wasn't a good time to confess that as an only child, I'd never actually slept in a bunk bed before.

"I'm Theodore Waverly," he said, reaching out a hand. "But most people call me Teddy."

I was immediately struck by his firm grip. I wondered if it was maybe something he'd learned from his dad or from watching people play presidents on TV.

"Hey, my best friend, Louisa, goes by her nickname, too," I replied. "Were you here last year? You might know her."

"Nope, this is my first time."

"Yeah, me too," I said. "Well, she's in the eighth-grade unit as well, and if this place is even half as cool as she says, I think we're gonna have a great summer."

"Here's hoping." He smiled.

"Oh, I'm Jack, by the way. Jack Goodrich."

"Nice to meet you, Jack Goodrich," he said, pronouncing the consonants in my name with precision. "Do you need some help with your bags?"

"No, my parents are unloading the car right now," I said, pointing my thumb to the door. "What about you?"

"Parents?" he asked. "No, I took the train from Chicago myself. They arranged for someone at the camp to pick me up from the station."

"Oh." I hesitated. "I meant bags. You good?"

"Right." Teddy nodded, frowning a bit. "Yes . . . I am good. Thanks."

When I met up with Lou again at the first-day cookout, she was with her bunkmate, a shy girl from Detroit, Michigan.

Enter Kaylee Cooper!

Kaylee spent the whole hour completely silent, shrinking into a baggy gray hoodie like she was trying to disappear. It wasn't until auditions later that day when she opened her mouth to sing and a *HUGE* belt voice rang out that we realized how special the person was hiding beneath that pile of gray fabric. Lou immediately became the president of her fan club and her cabin BFF, making sure Kaylee always felt included in camp activities.

Rehearsals for the end-of-camp showcase started the next morning. We wasted no time before we started piecing together a collection of songs and dances that we would perform for the entire camp on our final evening. Between rehearsals we'd wedge in dance classes, acting workshops, even stage-combat lessons, so by the time we made it to dinner, we were practically collapsing into our tater tots. What made it even better? Everyone here seemed to be just as Broadway-obsessed as Lou and me.

Things that would brand you a weirdo in Shaker Heights were just part of the daily routine at Camp Curtain Up. It wasn't uncommon to stumble upon an impromptu *Spring Awakening* sing-along or someone practicing Roxie Hart's monologue in an empty hallway. Kids gathered around campfires not to tell ghost stories but tales of doomed Broadway flops like *Carrie: The Musical* or *Bring Back Birdie*. If there was ever an argument, it was never over anything personal (there was just a lot to be said about which Elphaba *really* does the best riff in "The Wizard and I"). And when you passed two campers walking arm in arm, sharing a pair of earbuds, it didn't *necessarily* mean they were crushing on each other. (Most likely they were just listening to a Pasek and Paul power ballad.)

☆ ☆ ☆ ☆ ☆

"Let's play a game," Teddy announced to the mess hall on our third day of camp, wiping his fingers on his Lou Malnati's T-shirt. (In our seventy-two-hour friendship we'd only found one thing to disagree upon: As a New Yorker, I took pride in the fact that we not only invented musical theater but also made the best pizza. Teddy saw things differently, proclaiming the Chicago deep-dish to be the cuisine supreme . . . *you know, like a maniac.* Just to spite me, he'd taken to wearing a ratty T-shirt from his favorite pizza place, Lou Malnati's, even though it was oversize and covered with bleach stains.)

"What game?" Lou asked, looking up from her fruit salad.

"It's called Stephen Sondheim Sludge Bucket," Teddy declared.

"What?!" Kaylee giggled.

"It's easy," Teddy said, holding up a soup bowl. "You pass this around and everyone has to take a bite of food off their plate and add it to the bowl. And you *also* have to name a musical by the greatest composer of all time—Stephen Sondheim."

I knew I liked this guy.

"Once a title has been said, you can't repeat it. And if you can't think of one," he continued, now with a smirk, "you have to *eat* whatever's in the bowl!"

A chorus of *ewws* swept across the table.

"Aw man," Kaylee said, shrinking into her chair, stuffing her hands into her oversize hoodie. "I barely know any Stephen Sondheim shows."

"Well, in that case, why don't you start," said Teddy, handing her the empty bowl.

"Okay." Kaylee sighed, slithering a spaghetti noodle off her plate and into the ceremonial dish. "*Into the Woods*. Everyone knows that one."

Lou and I shared a sentimental look as she took the bowl from Kaylee and added a strawberry.

"*Sunday in the Park with George*."

"*Sweeney Todd*," a boy from my cabin announced, plopping a dollop of sour cream into the bowl.

"*Company*," a girl said, pouring in a splash of chocolate milk.

"*West Side Story*," another camper chimed in, adding a pickle.

"*Follies*"—a french fry.

"*Gypsy*"—an Oreo.

"*A Little Night Music*"—a hard-boiled egg yolk.

All around the table this continued, each Sondheim show becoming more and more obscure and each food item looking more and more unsavory. The next thing I knew, I was staring down at the pile of steaming slush, my mind drawing a complete blank.

"Uh-oh," Teddy jeered. "Have we actually stumped the great Jack Goodrich: Nerd King of Nerd Mountain?"

"Gimme a sec," I breathed.

"You got this, Jack!" Lou cheered from down the table.

Suddenly a lightbulb went off in my head. "*Saturday Night*!" I cried. "Sondheim's first musical." I handed Teddy the bowl triumphantly. "And one of the few shows he wrote that never made it to Broadway."

"Oh no," Kaylee whimpered, watching Teddy examine the garbage bowl. "The only other musical I knew was *Sweeney Todd.* If he gets even one more show, I'm gonna have to eat that, right?"

Lou frowned, patting her back sympathetically.

Teddy sighed, looking down at the bowl and then back up at Kaylee. "Well, I'm sorry to say . . ." He hesitated for a second. "That I will *not* be sharing this delicious meal with you, because I can't for the life of me think of a single one."

And with that, he plunged his spoon into the muck and scooped out a heaping pile of sludge.

"Ewwww!" the table erupted as he shoveled it into his mouth. *"Gross!"*

"Whatever." Teddy shrugged, chewing with his mouth open. "I always eat weird stuff to gross out my parents. It's just one of my things."

Kaylee hugged Lou in relief as Teddy scraped the remaining bites from the bowl.

It wasn't until that evening as I lay in the bunk above him that I realized there was *no way* Teddy was truly stumped. At his showcase audition on the first day, he sang "Everybody Says Don't," a tune from the little-known Sondheim musical *Anyone Can Whistle.*

☆ ☆ ☆ ☆ ☆

I hadn't realized how close Teddy, Kaylee, Lou, and I were getting until our counselors started calling us the Four Musketeers. It probably didn't help that by the end of the first week we'd taught ourselves the four-part harmony to Jason Robert Brown's "The New World," and would bust it out on walks and during games of capture the flag. Nor did it help that on the day our dance teacher taught us Bob Fosse's choreography to "All That Jazz," the four of us performed it at the dance mixer while the new Beyoncé song thumped in the background. And when showcase numbers were announced and Kaylee got assigned the difficult but showstopping song "He Wanted a Girl" from the musical *Giant*, we all crowded in a practice room so she could get comfortable singing to the three of us.

☆ ☆ ☆ ☆ ☆

Run-throughs turned into dress rehearsals, and as we neared the end of the second week of camp, we found ourselves backstage, sparked with the frenzy of another opening night. Counselors and campers from other units filed into the empty auditorium, eager to see what the eighth-graders had been rehearsing for the past two weeks. Duets gave way to solos and soon there was only one more number before I was set to perform. Lou and I had been paired to sing a beautiful song called "Runaways" from an obscure off-off-Broadway musical called *The Flood*. Under any other circumstance I would be frantically rehearsing with her in the dressing room, singing our lyrics double-time to make sure they were locked into our memories, but tonight I felt myself pulled by an invisible thread to the stage-right wing.

"Next on deck is Teddy Waverly, performing 'Why?' from *tick, tick... BOOM!*" our counselor Astrid said into her headset, alerting the backstage cast and crew.

I stood in the dark, watching as Teddy took his place on a stool downstage center, bathed in the yellow gleam of a follow spot. The sparse intro played as his gaze lifted upward, his eyes twinkling from the footlights. Despite being a total goofball offstage, tonight he seemed focused, almost freakishly relaxed. It felt like he was just sitting across from me at the mess hall, not in a five-hundred-seat theater, every ear listening in.

"He's really good, huh?" a voice said from behind me, causing me to practically jump out of my dress shoes.

"Sorry," Lou said, stifling a laugh, "I didn't mean to scare you."

"It's okay," I whispered. "I just didn't know you were there."

As Teddy moved into the bridge of the song, Lou squeezed in next to me to get a better view.

"With only so much time to spend

Don't wanna waste the time I'm given..."

"Think we'll all be here next year?" Lou asked.

"I dunno," I whispered, keeping my eyes fixed on Teddy. "I hope so."

As he arrived at the end of his song, he flipped into a sweet, clear falsetto for the final note. For a moment there was only silence, then the audience burst into resounding applause.

"We're next," Lou said, taking my hand. "You ready?"

"I think so," I said, giving her a squeeze.

From behind us, Astrid spoke in a low voice, calling a light cue into her headset. The blackout bloomed slowly into brightness, revealing a picnic blanket a stagehand had set up for us during the scene change. I turned to my friend one last time before our entrance.

"Thanks for convincing me to come here."

"Anytime," she whispered, stepping onstage and into the warm, comforting glow of a spotlight.

Louisa

"YAY!"

"You two are so good together!"

Kaylee and Teddy were waiting for me and Jack in the wings as we exited the stage, eagerly reaching out for hugs. Our duet from *The Flood* had gone really well. I was almost starting to take our onstage chemistry for granted, since we'd had so many opportunities over the past year to perform together. We could still hear the applause from the crowded auditorium, where furiously spinning ceiling fans did little to keep the sweltering heat at bay. It didn't matter, though—everyone was having such a good time cheering on their fellow campers that they barely noticed how hot it was.

"Thanks, guys!" Jack beamed. "And, Teddy, you were *awesome*."

"Totally," I chimed in. "We got to watch you from the wings before we went on. *So good!*"

"Yeah well, now Kaylee gets to wipe the floor with all of us," Teddy said with his lopsided smile. As if on cue, we suddenly heard Astrid, our favorite counselor, thanking everyone over the sound system for a "fabulous evening." There was one final number, she announced, and Jack, Teddy, and I simultaneously turned our attention to Kaylee, whose face instantly tightened in a nervous, but determined, expression.

"You ready?" I whispered, squeezing her arm. She nodded, then slowly, almost painfully, unzipped her gray hoodie and handed it to me like a turtle handing over its shell. Earlier that day, I'd had to work hard to convince her not to wear it onstage.

"I'll look fat without it," she'd fretted in our cabin, digging her hands into the hoodie's pockets and stretching it like a tarp in front of her. Even though I'd only known her for two weeks, I'd come to recognize this as her signature move.

"No you won't," I'd assured her, then tried my best to channel my friend Jenny Westcott's fashion sense by assembling an outfit that she'd feel comfortable wearing. As I looked at her now, I knew Jenny would be proud of my work. High-waisted jeans made her look taller and more mature, while a turquoise scoop-neck T-shirt looked lovely with her skin tone. Finally, some silver hoop earrings that we'd found buried in her suitcase would add a little sparkle around her face when the stage lights hit them just right.

"You're beautiful," I said, giving her arm one more squeeze. "Now go get 'em."

Jack and Teddy patted her back as she walked past us toward the stage. We all exchanged a look, anticipating the thrill of her performance.

"I already have chills, and she hasn't even started singing yet," whispered Jack. Teddy and I both nodded in agreement as the accompanist began to play Michael John LaChiusa's gorgeous introduction, and tears immediately sprung to my eyes as Kaylee's one-of-a-kind voice floated through the auditorium:

"He wanted a girl who hates dusty roads
He wanted a girl who cries porcelain tears . . ."

Kaylee's voice was pure magic; it seemed to come out of every pore in her body, not just her mouth. As shy as she had been on the first day of camp, she was now in utter command of the auditorium, singing with heartrending emotion about unrequited love. When she finished the song, it took everything in our power not to rush the stage like crazy fans rushing the field at a sporting event. Instead, the three of us grabbed one another's hands and jumped up and down, shrieking with pride. With each jump, I recalled thinking last year that nothing could beat my first year at Camp Curtain Up. But the formation of the Four Musketeers this year had proven me wrong. How the heck was I going to make it through the good-byes in the morning?

☆ ☆ ☆ ☆ ☆

"We just have to stay in touch to remind each other all the time how special it was."

The show was over, and Kaylee and I were walking toward the big end-of-camp bonfire, discussing how we were going to manage our post-CCU sadness. The air outside was much cooler than inside the auditorium, which meant Kaylee was once again wearing her gray hoodie, happy and safe inside her zippered security blanket. But now, instead of digging her hands into her pockets, she hooked one arm through mine, while her other hand held a flashlight, its beam of light dancing across the uneven path in front of us.

"Deal," I said, leaning into her shoulder. "Let's start a 'Four Musketeers' group text after we leave tomorrow."

We found Jack and Teddy already sitting on a log by the bonfire, animatedly chatting about something. This had become a familiar sight over the past two weeks. They just never seemed to run out of things to talk about.

"Aren't you two sick of each other yet?" I joked as we approached.

"Oh, we are," Teddy deadpanned. "We just don't want to hurt each other's feelings."

Kaylee and I rolled our eyes.

"You guys," she said, shoving Teddy's shoulder, "move over. Make room for us."

"Oooh," teased Jack, "give the star a showstopping finale and suddenly she's the boss of everybody."

"Oh my God, shut up," Kaylee said, instantly

embarrassed. She still wasn't used to being referred to as a star.

As the boys scooted over on the log, allowing us to join them, Teddy cleared his throat in that I-have-something-important-to-talk-about way.

"So, Lou," Teddy said, a somewhat accusatory tone in his voice, "what we were actually talking about before you got here is very serious. I just found out that you and Jack have never heard of the Ghostlight Festival."

Before I could even respond, Kaylee grabbed my arm, aghast.

"Wait, hold up—you don't know what *Ghostlight* is?"

I turned questioningly to Jack, who shook his head and shrugged.

"Looks like we have some explaining to do, Lou."

"Sorry, guys," I ventured, cautiously, "I don't know what you're talking about."

Kaylee and Teddy exchanged a look like I'd just said I didn't know the difference between an up-tempo and a ballad.

"Apparently we've been living under a rock," Jack said, prompting Teddy to nod aggressively.

"A big rock," he confirmed, "a boulder, a mountain . . ."

"All right, all right!" I interrupted. "How 'bout instead of making fun of us for being clueless, you explain what Ghostlight *is*?"

"Sorry," Kaylee said, giggling. "It's just—you know—I assumed you would have heard of it, 'cause, like . . . you guys are the biggest MTNs here."

"In case you forgot, MTN stands for Musical Theater Nerd," Teddy added, poking Jack's foot with a stick. Before Jack could react, Kaylee succeeded in grabbing the focus back with the sheer volume of her voice.

"Okay, so here's the deal!" she explained, "Ghostlight is this big theater competition that happens over one weekend in the fall, and a bunch of schools from around the Midwest enter with, like, shorter versions of musicals."

"Which is perfect, since Jack and Lou are both short," Teddy quipped.

"Oh my God, I bet you couldn't be serious if someone *paid* you!" Kaylee shrieked with exasperation, sending some unseen creature scurrying into the brush behind us.

"Careful, Kaylee," warned Teddy. "Your voice

could send all the little squirrels and chipmunks into cardiac arrest."

"You're just jealous of her vocal placement," Jack said.

"We're *all* jealous of her vocal placement," I chimed in, making Kaylee squirm self-consciously.

"Can I continue, *please*?" Kaylee asked, planting her hands on her hips.

"Yes, please," I urged, then turned to shush the boys.

"Okay," she went on. "So kids do these thirty-minute presentations of shows, like *Godspell*, or *Hairspray*, or *South Pacific*—"

"—and what's awesome," Teddy interjected, "is that students direct them."

"Wait—how does that work?" asked Jack, perking up. "Who decides which kid gets to direct?"

"Well, there's a teacher who supervises," Teddy explained. "Usually the drama teacher—"

"Or the science teacher who does drama after school, if you go to a school like Rustin Middle instead of Cavendish Prep," Kaylee interrupted, adopting a strong urban accent as she pronounced the name of her school, then a posh British accent when she pronounced Teddy's. We all liked to make fun of Teddy for going to a rich-kid school. He didn't seem to mind, though—he had a good sense of humor about it.

"Whatever," said Teddy, rolling his eyes. "Some *grown-up* is there to, like, guide and support while a student—"

"—usually an eighth-grader—"

"—directs it, and then at the festival, each school presents their show, the judges fill out these scorecards, and at the awards ceremony on the last day—"

"*—Teddy's school wins!*" Kaylee announced, catching Teddy off guard.

"What?"

"Please!" Kaylee threw him her most incredulous look.

"When's the last time Cavendish *lost*? Ten years ago?"

"No!" Teddy blurted out defensively, then offered more quietly, "Eleven."

"For real?! Okay, so, like, they haven't lost in over a decade," Kaylee continued, leaning in toward me and Jack. "Meanwhile my school? Never even made it into the top ten. So of *course* Teddy thinks Ghostlight is 'awesome.' The rest of the schools basically go to see *how* they'll win, not *if*."

She dug her hands into the pockets of her hoodie, smiling smugly at Teddy. I glanced at him only to find that he, for once, had no witty comeback. Rather than let him off the hook, Jack and I dug in even more.

"Well, I'd love anything that let me win *every time*," Jack said mischievously.

"Yeah, sounds like a real blast, this Ghostlight thing," I said sarcastically. "Kaylee, why doesn't your school skip all the hard work and just give Cavendish the trophy now?"

"Exactly," said Kaylee. "As my dad likes to say, '*The game is rigged*.'"

"All right, all right," said Teddy, throwing his hands up in surrender, "I see where this is going. But it's not like I had anything to do with them winning. I only competed in Ghostlight for the first time last year, and I had a really small part."

There was a brief pause as we all waited for him to continue. Teddy took a breath, then looked at us sheepishly and announced with a sigh, "I was the Fiddler."

"As in the *Fiddler on the Roof*?!" I exclaimed. Teddy quickly turned from sheepish to full-blown embarrassed (because despite the show's title, the actual fiddler wasn't really a role).

"Look—the kid who directed it thought it would be cool if I stood on a box upstage in profile for the whole presentation," he sputtered. "Ya know . . . symbolically."

By the time he said the word *symbolically* the three of us were doubled over with laughter.

"Whatever!" he protested. "We *won*!"

It was one of those nights you never want to end. Jokes turned into comedy routines, moments became instant memories, and promises of everlasting friendship were made over and over again. But once the bonfire died down and other campers started shuffling back to their bunks, I began to feel sad, silently acknowledging that it was almost time to leave. It was too soon for tears—I'd have plenty of time for those in the morning—so instead I just stared wistfully into the glowing embers. After a few minutes of quiet, Kaylee stretched her arms above her head and let out a big yawn.

"Yo, I'm beat, you guys," she said. "I gotta go to sleep."

"Me too," I said, rising to my feet. I turned to Teddy and Jack, who remained seated on the log, their faces only partly lit by the fading glow of the fire.

"You wanna walk with us? Kaylee's got a flashlight."

The boys exchanged a look, and I don't know why—but I suddenly had the sense that they were waiting for the other one to respond.

"Um," Teddy said finally, looking down at his feet, "I'm gonna hang here a little longer, I think."

I looked at Jack, who glanced first at Teddy, then at me.

"Yeah," he said, tugging at the bottom of his sweatshirt. "Me too, I think."

"All right, well, don't get attacked by a bear," Kaylee cautioned with a smile, clicking on her flashlight and heading off into the darkness. I hesitated as I realized that this moment marked the unofficial end of camp. Tomorrow would be nothing but one long good-bye.

"Okay, then—night, you guys," I said, brushing bits of bark off the back of my jeans. "Great job tonight."

"You too," they sang out in unison, Teddy extending his arm toward me with a congratulatory thumbs-up.

As I turned to follow Kaylee, her flashlight beam already far ahead of me, I couldn't help but think that my innocent question—"You wanna walk with us?"—had somehow put Teddy and Jack on the spot. A new, strange thought started to creep into my head, but I was too tired, too sad, too full of emotion about my friends and my time at CCU to give it much attention. *I'm probably wrong, anyway,* I thought, scampering across the rocky path to catch up with Kaylee, *they're just two friends who aren't tired yet.*

Jack

THE FORECAST FOR OUR LAST day at Camp Curtain Up may have been bright and sunny, but on the girls' end of camp, it was showers with a chance of Kleenex. I had never been great with good-byes, but I felt heartless by comparison when Teddy and I joined Kaylee and Lou for our final send-off. Lou's face was red and puffy from what looked like hours of crying, and Kaylee's pockets were overflowing with soggy, crumpled tissues. To be fair, I shouldn't have been entirely surprised; Lou had been extremely sentimental on the closing nights of both *Guys and Dolls* and *Into the Woods*, but even I had never seen her this distraught.

"Get ahold of yourself, Lululemon," Teddy joked as he hugged Lou tightly. "It's the twenty-first century. You can find us anywhere, anytime."

"He's right," said Kaylee, choking back her own sobs. "So give me one more hug and then text me in, like, twenty minutes."

"Our parents wanna get going, Lou," I said, suppressing my desire to make a crack about needing Dylan, the lifeguard, to report for duty if her waterworks continued. "Both our dads are stressing out about traffic."

"Okay," Lou said, giving both Teddy and Kaylee a final hug, leaving little wet patches on their shoulders. "Bye, you guys!"

We watched Lou's funeral march to the parking lot, her shoulders still quivering from the sobs. I could almost hear a violin playing in the distance.

"Is she gonna be okay?" Kaylee asked, looking practically pulled together in comparison.

"Almost definitely." I smiled.

"Okay, I should go, too," she moaned, reaching out and wrapping her arms around Teddy and me in a kind of double hug.

"Teddy, I'll see you in the fall," she said optimistically. "And, Jack . . . I'll see you on our text thread."

"Bye, Kaylee!" We waved as she followed in Lou's footsteps toward the parking lot.

I turned back to Teddy. He raised his shoulders and gave me the same crooked smile I saw on that first day when he offered up his top bunk.

"Well . . . I guess it's that time, Jack," he said. "My parents probably want to get going."

"Yeah, totally," I said, looking back to my family's minivan. "That's awesome your mom and dad came. I thought you were taking the train home."

"Oh, my mom found out there was good *antiquing* in Kalamazoo, so they figured they might as well pick me up on the way back." Teddy rolled his eyes. "Sorry you didn't get to meet them. My dad's on a conference call, and my mom is, like, deathly afraid of nature."

"Some other time," I said, stuffing my hands in my pockets and looking to the ground.

It was so weird. For the past few days, I'd been looking for any excuse to get a few seconds alone with Teddy. I wasn't even sure what I'd say to him—I guess I'd been hoping that things would just present themselves "organically," like in our improv workshop: *"Yes, and . . ."* We shuffled aimlessly, staring at shoes that had become filthy with dust, mud, and grass stains over the past two weeks. It felt like the night before at the campfire all over again—Lou and Kaylee leaving us alone, only for me and Teddy to find ourselves at a total loss for words.

"Is your drive back home very long?" Teddy asked, finally breaking the silence.

"About four hours. Five if we stop for food."

"Cool." He nodded.

"Um, what about you?" I asked.

"Actually, I'm not sure," he said, furrowing his brow. "Probably a little less."

"Cool," I echoed, looking back down at the grass.

He dug his toe into the dirt for a second before speaking up.

"Well, I'm glad we—"

"Theodore!" a woman's voice cut him off.

I turned to see a tall woman walking toward us. She had thick black hair and was wearing a crisp blouse and red pants with a crease down the center sharp enough to slice through a scone. She wore a string of pearls around her neck and matching earrings. Her heels were tall and white, conspicuously out of place on a grassy field. This could only be one person.

"It's time to go," Teddy's mom told him.

"I thought Dad was on a call?" Teddy responded.

"Well, he was, but they're in London and it was getting late, so he had to wrap it up," she said airily. "We should head out now if we want to get back to Evanston before it gets dark."

"Okay." He nodded. "This is my friend Jack," he said, gesturing to me.

"How do you do, Jack," she said with a wave of her hand, in a way that made me not quite sure whether she actually wanted to know how I was doing. Her fingernails were smooth and polished with painted white tips at the end. Her eyes met mine for a quick second and then went immediately back to her son. I took this to mean that I wouldn't be shaking hands and regaling her with camp stories.

"I'm going back to the car," she said, pointing a manicured nail toward the parking lot. "If you want to say good-bye to your friend, I'll have your dad pull the car around."

"Oh, Mom, wait!" Teddy said, giving a wily grin. "I just remembered—I need to grab my jar of tomato worms. I left them in the cabin, and I'm thinking of building a terrarium for them in the basement."

"Ugh." She shuddered. "Please tell me you're joking, Theodore. Those are not coming in the car with us."

"Okay." He shrugged. "Well, I'll be there in a second, then."

And with that, she turned and began teetering back to the parking lot, her heels sinking into the grass with every step.

"Have you really been collecting tomato worms?" I asked once his mom was out of earshot.

"Sick, no!" He laughed. "Those things are nasty—but did you see her face?"

He flashed a smile at me for a second, before turning his gaze to the parking lot.

"I should go," he said.

"Yeah, me too."

I reached out for a handshake but felt his stomach crunch into my arm. *Oh, we're going in for a hug. Of course, you idiot.* His arm reached around my back and did a kind of double pat on my shoulder blade. We pulled out of it awkwardly, avoiding eye contact.

"Okay . . . see ya," I said, and started off toward my van.

"See ya," he echoed.

It only took a few steps to realize that we were, of course, walking in the same direction, but because we had already said "good-bye," we continued in silence. The only sound was our tennis shoes, treading softly on the grass.

We paused once we got to the parking lot, where my parents were loading the last of my things into our minivan and Teddy's mom was waving impatiently next to a sleek silver sedan.

"Well . . . ," I said, not sure what to say.

"Bye, Jack," Teddy said, in a tone I couldn't quite decipher. With that, he took off toward his mom, leaving me at the edge of the parking lot, unsure of what to think.

"Bye, Teddy," I said, to no one but myself.

☆ ☆ ☆ ☆ ☆

I could still remember the exact moment I realized what it meant to be "gay." I had just finished a performance of *Mary Poppins* and was bouncing down the stairs from my dressing room to meet my mom at the stage door. When I made it to the landing, I caught sight of one of my favorite cast members, Charlie, greeting a group of friends who had just seen the show. Charlie was one of the younger men in our cast, a floppy-haired dancer who played Neleus, the statue who comes to life in "Jolly Holiday." Charlie was popular with all the kids in the cast because he would always bring baked goods to the theater—salted caramel brownies and coconut macaroons and red velvet cupcakes made in his apartment kitchen. Everyone in the cast would groan as he pushed through the stage door on Sunday matinees, his cheeks rosy and arms loaded with Tupperware containers.

Oh no, Charlie! What are you torturing us with this time? the chorus girls would moan as he passed their dressing rooms, the smell of chocolate rich and tempting in the cramped halls.

"They're only *pretending* they don't want those cookies," my wrangler had to explain to me, rolling his eyes. "Trust me, by 'Step in Time,' those cookies will be gone quicker than a pair of free house seats to *Wicked*."

I hesitated in the stairwell, watching as Charlie hugged one of his stage-door friends, a man with a scruffy beard and thick black-rimmed glasses. The scruffy man grabbed Charlie by the shoulders and kissed him on the lips. Charlie then reached down and took his hand, laughing as he pushed through the metal stage door and into the heavy crowds of 41st Street.

My feet froze on the rubberized stairs. Charlie kissed that guy the way my uncle Bill kissed my aunt Linda on their wedding day, or how my dad would kiss my mom after returning from a long weekend at a city-planning conference. The next day when I mentioned the stage-door encounter to McKenzie, the oldest of our Jane Bankses, she shrugged it off, barely looking up from her iPad.

"Oh yeah, you didn't know? Charlie is totes gay."

"Totes gay," I mumbled. I guessed that meant that you were a boy and wanted to kiss another boy the way Mr. Banks kisses Mrs. Banks, or Harold Hill kisses Marian the Librarian, or basically every leading man kisses his costar nightly on every stage in our ten-block radius.

I stared at the new text message on my phone screen.

TEDDY: ***I'M STARTING THIS GROUP THREAD RIGHT NOW SO KAYLEE AND LOU DON'T HAVE PANIC ATTACKS ON THEIR CAR RIDE HOME.***

I leaned my head against the car window, the glass cool on my cheek. Thoughts raced through my head like cars on the interstate. I tried on each idea like a back-to-school outfit.

Why couldn't I stop thinking about Teddy Waverly?

Maybe I'm just not used to having "guy friends."

Is this what having a new best friend is supposed to feel like?

I found myself thinking back to Charlie and his scruffy-faced boyfriend.

But did I really want to kiss Teddy?

The phone buzzed again in my palm.

TEDDY: *ALSO I JUST LET OUT THE SICKEST BELCH EVER. I'M PRETTY SURE I COULD TASTE SOME OF THAT STEPHEN SONDHEIM SLUDGE BUCKET FROM LAST WEEK.*

Yeah, nope. Definitely didn't want to kiss him.

Well, if I don't want to kiss him, I thought to myself, *then I'm probably not gay.*

My phone vibrated again. This time gray writing appeared beneath Teddy's message.

Kaylee Cooper has named the conversation "The Four Musketeers."

KAYLEE: *I CHANGED OUR GROUP NAME ;) LUV U GUYS!!!*

Bzzz

LOU: *OMG THE FOUR MUSKETEERS! ALSO I MISS YOU GUYS SOOOOOOO MUCH.*

MISS YOU GUYS TOO, I typed. *HOPE EVERYONE HAS A GOOD TRIP BACK.*

Send.

My mom lowered the volume on the car radio.

"That sweet boy you introduced us to—Teddy, was it?" she said, looking over her shoulder. "Was he one of your good friends at camp?"

"Um, yeah," I said, adjusting the seat belt that suddenly felt like it was cutting into my neck. "Yeah, him and Lou and that girl Kaylee were kind of my best friends."

"Well, that's great," my mom said, looking over to my dad. "It's nice to see you making friends with some boys. I know in Shaker Heights it hasn't always been the easiest."

"Well, I mean I'm good friends with Sebastian and Adam and, like, a lot of the boys from the soccer team," I responded somewhat defensively.

"Right, right," my mom agreed. "I just mean, it's good that you're making friends with boys who have the same interests as you."

"Uh-huh," I replied flatly.

"I'm just happy to see that you're happy, is all." She smiled, turning back around and reaching for the volume nob.

Bzzz, my phone vibrated in my hand.

LOU: 350 DAYS, 7 HOURS AND 13 MINUTES UNTIL CAMP CURTAIN UP

"Hold your breath," my dad announced to the car. "We're about to cross the state line into Ohio."

I filled my lungs with air as a blue-and-white sign breezed overhead, the state motto challenging me with its cursive writing—

"Ohio: So Much to Discover."

After a minute, a green mile-marker sign zipped by on the side of our minivan, marking our first stretch into my home state. We all let out dramatically loud gushes of air just as my phone vibrated once again.

KAYLEE: WELL AT LEAST I'LL GET TO WATCH TEDDY WIN AT GHOSTLIGHT :P

I knew it was foolish, but in that moment the only thing I could feel was jealousy. Even losing horribly to Teddy still meant getting to hang out with him. Without fully realizing it, my fingers took over and began gliding across the screen of my phone. They closed out the text thread and clicked on the web browser icon. At this point I knew it was probably pointless, but curiosity had gotten the better of me. I typed into the search bar:

"Ghostlight Festival dates?"

☆☆☆☆☆

We pulled up to our driveway in the Sussex Meadows subdivision, the air filled with the buzz of cicadas. I flung open the car door and bounced out onto the asphalt, the idea of a theater competition flickering in my head. Sure, it maybe wasn't totally fair and Teddy's school would probably win again, but if we got to see our friends, what would it matter? And it's not like we had anything else to do except wait around for our director, Belinda Grier, to announce our spring musical.

"Dennis, if you want to start unloading the car, I'll go switch on the AC," my mom called to my dad, unlocking the front door.

I carried my backpack and dance bag into the house, immediately struck by the familiar lemon scent. Sometimes it took a couple weeks away to realize what things actually made me think of home. I made my way up the stairs, flicking every light switch I passed, and dumped my bags on the floor of my bedroom. In anticipation of my return, someone had decided to make my bed—a truly rare sight, which I hoped was not a hint. I walked back downstairs to unload the rest of my stuff from the trunk, but was shocked to find my neighbor standing in my driveway, a mischievous grin on her face.

"Whoa," I muttered. "I was just about to call you."

"Aw," Lou said, her hands clasped behind her back. "You miss me already?"

"Ha." I bounced down the stairs.

"Well, *this* will make you feel better," she trumpeted. From behind her back she drew a rustling newspaper. It was opened to a half-page black-and-white ad, the graphic of a snowcapped mountain with a swirl of music notes looping around it. In big letters across the top, it read clearly:

"*The Heights Are Alive!* The Shaker Heights Players Proudly Announce Auditions for Our Fall Musical: *The Sound of Music*."

Louisa

"Wow," said Jack, blinking at the newspaper in my hand, "welcome home."

"Right?!" I said gleefully, hopping from the dark lawn onto his stoop. "I was sure the Players were going to do a show with no kids, but instead they're doing a show that's, like, all *about* kids!"

I couldn't believe it. I'd spent the ride back from camp dabbing my eyes and blowing my nose, obsessively texting "The Four Musketeers" pathetic messages like ***Let's just go back!*** and ***I miss us!*** By the time we pulled into our driveway, I'd used up every tissue my mom had provided, plus half a dozen rough paper napkins from the burger place we passed near Coldwater. I was totally prepared to spend my evening watching television with my parents in a funk of self-pity, so you can imagine how I felt when the first thing that greeted me upon my return was the *Sun Press* delivering the news that the Shaker Heights Players would be doing *The Sound of Music* in the fall. It was like the theater gods had once again heard my cries and given me a perfect coming-home present. I couldn't wait for Jack to get home so I could share our good fortune.

"They announced it early this year," Jack said, taking the newspaper from me and studying it closely.

"I know—gives us more time to prepare!"

"Oh—you wanna audition for it?" He looked up with a wry smile.

"Ha-ha," I said, snatching the paper away and swatting his arm with it. "Very funny!"

I dropped the newspaper on the ground and grabbed his hand, forcing him into a waltz around his front lawn.

"Raindrops on roses and whiskers on kittens . . ."

"Long time no see, Lou," Mr. Goodrich called out as he walked past us carrying Jack's heaviest duffel bag. "Don't you want a break from all that singing and dancing?"

"Never, Mr. Goodrich!" I shouted back, twirling Jack around and around.

"Help!" Jack cried out in mock despair. "I've been hijacked by a musical number!"

"What's going on, you two?" Mrs. Goodrich asked, emerging from behind their car with Jack's sleeping bag.

"The Players are doing SoundOfMusic *this fa-all,"* I sang out, squishing the words together to fit the melody of "My Favorite Things."

"Ooh, what a classic!" Mrs. Goodrich said, and without hesitation joined in the song, pretending Jack's sleeping bag was her waltz partner.

"Brown paper packages tied up with string," she and I sang, *"these are a few of my favorite things!"*

"Dad, help!" Jack cried out again.

"Hey, Von Trapp family, keep it down." Mr. Goodrich re-emerged from the house, laughing, "It's Sunday night and *some people* might want to enjoy a little peace and quiet before their work week begins." As he gestured toward the neighboring houses, we all stopped twirling and stumbled backward, dizzy and slightly out of breath.

"*Thank you*," Jack gasped, bending over and clutching his knees for balance.

"You're right." Mrs. Goodrich sighed. "Our neighbors might not be as entertained as we'd like them to be. But hey—this is very exciting, Lou. Thanks for sharing the news. There's just one more bag, Jack. Can you bring it in?" she asked, walking into the house.

"Yup, I got it," Jack replied. I followed him to the car, my initial excitement giving way to strategy.

"Okay, so I'm thinking I'll go for Brigitta, since she's the feistiest one," I stated, referring to the role I thought I could play in *The Sound of Music*, "and even though you're a little young, I think you should go for Friedrich."

Jack furrowed his brow.

"Really?"

"Yes, *really*. I mean, you're definitely closer in age to Friedrich than to Kurt."

"What if I'm not right for either one of the boys?" he asked, approaching the trunk.

I was surprised by this sudden doubt coming from my friend. It was as if he'd forgotten how good he was or something.

"Don't be ridiculous!" I said, leaning on the side of the car. "I mean, maybe if they were doing this on Broadway? But the Players never get enough boys to audition for their shows, and since they know you from *Into the Woods*, it's hard to imagine that they wouldn't cast you. Plus, you don't look *that* young anymore. I think that if you stood up really straight—which you'd *have to anyway as a Von Trapp kid*—you could totally pass for fourteen . . ."

I thought for sure he'd throw me a look for teasing him about his height, but instead he responded with a halfhearted, "Yeah, maybe."

I followed his gaze into the trunk, where one overstuffed tote bag remained.

"Hey," I said, pointing to a crumpled red wad of fabric with bleach spots peeking out from a corner of the bag, "isn't that Teddy's T-shirt?"

"Yep," Jack murmured, gently pulling it out to reveal the logo of Lou Malnati's, Teddy's favorite deep-dish pizza place in Chicago. He started to smile. "That jerk."

"You mean you didn't *know* it was in your bag?" I squealed. Jack shook his head, and we both started to laugh.

Looked like Teddy had won this round of their heated debate over New York vs. Chicago-style pizza. As our laughter subsided, I turned to face Jack, who held a curious expression.

"You okay?" I asked.

Startled, Jack blinked a few times, then hastily grabbed the tote bag, stuffing the T-shirt deep inside.

"Yeah, totally," he replied, "I'm just thinking about how I can get him back." He slammed the trunk shut and headed toward his house. The same strange thought that I'd had the night before started to creep into my brain again, as I remembered the look he and Teddy shared when I'd asked them if they wanted to walk with me and Kaylee. In the year that I'd known Jack, he'd never talked about liking someone—you know, in a crush way. It was hard to imagine him talking about anyone, let alone a boy (let alone *Teddy*—who loved describing farts and voluntarily ate sludge with a spoon!). And I certainly wasn't going to ask. Besides, there were other subjects that were much easier and much more fun to discuss, like our future theatrical adventures.

"So, hey—you wanna come over and watch

Sound of Music tomorrow? No point in waiting, right?" I called after him.

"Um, maybe," he said, opening the screen door to his house, "I told my mom I'd help her with chores and stuff, since I've been away for two weeks and everything. But maybe tomorrow night?"

"Okay, great!" I chirped. "Let me know if you're free."

"Will do," he said, letting the screen door shut behind him. I skipped across Jack's lawn to the sidewalk, the pulse of the summer crickets providing accompaniment as I hummed the rest of "My Favorite Things" on my walk home.

☆ ☆ ☆ ☆ ☆

The next day my mom had plans for me, too, insisting that in order to "avoid the lines," we needed to get my back-to-school shopping out of the way. By three thirty we'd loaded up on school supplies, new jeans, packets of socks and underwear and hair ties, plus a new fall jacket. We were now (finally) wrapping up our outing with a trip to the shoe department at Macy's, where I waited on a bench for the salesman to bring me a variety of choices in—ugh—size four and a half.

Mom was wandering aimlessly around the nearby cosmetics counters in a shopped-out daze, so I seized the opportunity to check my "Four Musketeers" text thread. I'd texted earlier to tell them about *The Sound of Music*, and an assortment of predictably amusing reactions were waiting for me.

KAYLEE: SOUND OF MUSIC?!? OMG, SO FUN!

TEDDY: LET ME GUESS LOU . . . BRIGITTA?

JACK: UR A GENIUS.

KAYLEE: WHAT ABOUT U JACK?

JACK: LOU SAYS I CAN PLAY FRIEDRICH IF I STAND UP STRAIGHT.

KAYLEE: OMG, FOR REALS? LOL!

TEDDY: JACK I THINK U SHOULD B TOTALLY HUNCHED OVER + WALK W/ A LIMP. DARE 2 B DIFFERENT.

My fingers were poised and ready to text a witty retort when a shadow fell across my phone's screen. A voice behind me, deeper than I remembered but nonetheless unmistakable, made my hand freeze in midair.

"I think it's the *Three* Musketeers, Benning."

A pair of the biggest sneakers I'd ever seen landed with a thud on the floor next to my dainty sandals as Tanner Falzone's gigantic frame stepped over the bench and plunked down next to me. My mind scrambled, searching in desperation for a clever comeback (I'd had plenty in mind for my text thread—why was I suddenly at a loss?). But like any good predator, Tanner understood that the element of surprise was key to taking down its prey. Caught in his grip, I was momentarily speechless. All I could do was turn my phone over in my lap and hope he didn't have another zinger ready to go.

"What's up?" he asked, flashing a grin that made me feel the same funny feeling I'd experienced last spring when he chased me down after a fateful *Guys and Dolls* rehearsal. In one brief encounter, he'd gone from being a bully I tried to avoid at all costs to someone who, quite unexpectedly, had made it clear he was (at least in that moment) on my side. Needless to say, for the rest of seventh grade, things had been a little weird between us. I couldn't dismiss him as easily as I once had because he'd been (*gulp*) nice to me, and I think for the same reason, Tanner didn't quite know how to act around me, either. Jack, of course, *loved* to tease me about Tanner, insisting that he liked me, which made me feel even more uncomfortable around him. After an entire summer without seeing each other, I'd hoped whatever awkwardness had existed between us would have disappeared. Now, as I fidgeted nervously on the shoe-store bench, I realized with dread that while Tanner seemed to have gotten over the awkwardness, *I clearly had not.*

"Not much," I answered flatly, unsure as to whether he was actually looking for an answer. "Shoe shopping."

"Yeah, same," he said, scanning the walls of footwear. "Good thing we're in the shoe department."

"Yeah." Once again, I could think of nothing to say. He'd said something funny, and all I could come up with was "Yeah"? I was an actress! Why couldn't I pick up my cues?

Inside my head was a tiny Lou screaming at me to say something hilarious. But I was too distracted by how much taller Tanner had gotten over the summer, and by the way he'd let his hair grow out. As if reading my mind, he raked his fingers through his hair, pushing shaggy strands off his forehead.

"You do any plays this summer?" he asked.

"Um, well, not exactly," I replied, trying to sound casual, "but Jack and I just got back from a theater camp yesterday."

Tanner smirked.

"They have theater camps?"

"Yeah, they're really fun."

"Is that where the 'Four Musketeers' are from?" he asked, gesturing toward my phone.

I nodded, wondering just how much of my text thread he'd actually seen.

"Mm-hm."

A moment of silence passed, and I realized it was my turn to ask him a question. Acting like a normal human engaged in a normal conversation had never been so challenging.

"Um, you went to soccer camp, right?"

A look of surprise crossed Tanner's face—maybe because he wasn't expecting me to know what he'd done over the summer.

"Yeah," he said. "It was cool. I broke a kid's nose."

My horrified reaction forced him to add hastily, "Not on purpose, it just happened while we were scrimmaging."

"Oh." My ignorance of soccer terms must have been fairly obvious, because Tanner went on to explain, "A scrimmage is like a friendly game."

"Yeah, until you break someone's nose."

Finally! The tiny Lou inside my head leaped and cheered. I knew I'd gained points by the way Tanner chuckled approvingly.

"Well . . . I guess so," he said, grabbing his Godzilla-size sneakers from the floor and lurching off the bench. "All right, Benning, see you back at school. Hope they've got some doll shoes in the back for ya." He cocked his head toward my tiny feet and let out a snort.

"Ha-ha," I replied, then stared after him as he sauntered toward the checkout counter, where his mom stood waiting, credit card in hand. My phone chiming snapped me to attention, and I turned it over to read the latest texts from the Musketeers.

JACK: *LOU WOULD MAKE SURE I WALKED W/ A LIMP IN REAL LIFE IF I SABOTAGED AN AUDITION.*

KAYLEE: *LOU, R U JUST GONNA LET US TALK ABOUT U LIKE THIS?*

TEDDY: *MAYBE SHE'LL ONLY TEXT BACK IF WE CALL HER BRIGITTA.*

JACK: *SHE'S PROBABLY HIKING THE ALPS RIGHT NOW 2 PREPARE.*

Teddy: *Whatvr she's doing must b pretty important if she's going 2 ignore the 4 Musketeers!*

Kaylee: *What could b more important than us???*

I glanced up as Tanner and his mom wandered away from the shoe department, still feeling a little buzzy from our encounter. The thought of seeing him back at school made me both nervous and—I couldn't believe it—a little excited. My fingers shaking slightly, I finally typed back:

Me: *Nothing's more important than u guys! Sorry! I'm just doing some shoe shopping!*

Jack

IF THE FIRST DAY OF SCHOOL after summer vacation is a shock, then the first day of school the year that you become an eighth-grader is like sticking your finger in an outlet. Walking into school with Lou by my side, I felt like a kid sneaking into a PG-13 movie. Girls who were my height just last May now looked like mini-adults, wearing makeup and towering disinterestedly over the sixth-graders. Boys whose voices cracked reading oral reports in seventh grade now sounded like leading men in police procedurals, making wisecracks as they were forced to remove their snapback hats. Some kids had gotten braces. Others had gotten them off. Even though my parents swore I'd gotten taller over the summer, I sure didn't feel like it today.

Thankfully, there was one person who had grown even less than me—Lou, and we were lucky enough to be placed in the same homeroom. We took our seats and listened as our classmates tried to top one another, bragging about their summer adventures. Sebastian Maroney had gone to soccer camp. Brooklyn Brown went horseback riding. Sarah Fineberg, our General Cartwright from *Guys and Dolls*, had spent most of the summer on a fishing trip with her dad.

As we waited for our homeroom teacher, Mr. McGuire, to arrive, the figure of a tall woman appeared in the doorway. She wore espadrille wedges, a denim skirt, and big dark sunglasses.

"Is that a new student?" I leaned over to ask Lou.

"Oh, no." Lou smiled. "That's Jenny."

I couldn't believe my eyes. I hadn't seen her since she'd left for her dance intensive at Cincinnati Ballet two months earlier, and it was clear that her technique was not the only thing that had grown over the summer.

"Have you not been following her Instagram?" Lou inquired. "Yeah, she grew, like, five inches. She's a real prima ballerina now."

Jenny strutted over to us, lifting her sunglasses and resting them on her head.

"Hey, you two," she said, sliding into the desk in front of us. Despite being a graceful dancer, she still looked awkward stuffing her long limbs into the desk clearly intended for a smaller student.

"How was Cincinnati Ballet?" I asked.

"It was *everything*," she said, shifting her body to face us. "I can't believe I have to come back to *school*. I mean, I already know I want to be a principal dancer at the American Ballet Theatre when I grow up. Why do I have to take math? Ballerinas only have to count up to eight."

"Yeah, until you have to do your taxes," I replied.

"Wait, what?" she asked.

"Never mind," I mumbled.

"Lou told me you had a great time at camp," Jenny said, folding up her sunglasses. But before I could respond, Mr. McGuire walked into the room. He launched into the usual first-day-of-school business—course syllabus, when after-school sign-ups would be posted, which of us had lucked out and got the early lunch period. While the excitement of meeting new teachers and cracking open fresh textbooks kept me engaged for a little bit, I still felt my mind drifting back to Camp Curtain Up and my friends who were embarking on their first days of school as well.

As the bell rang, my classmates and I poured into the hallway.

"Lou, do you want to come with me to the girls' room?" Jenny said, more as a statement than a question. Lou didn't even have time to answer. Jenny was already dragging her down the hallway, disappearing into the sea of new backpacks. I had no choice but to kill some time at my locker, unloading my math textbook and pulling my cell phone out of the inside pocket of my jacket.

"2 New Messages from The Four Musketeers," flashed a notification on my screen.

KAYLEE: HAPPY FIRST DAY OF SCHOOL, YOU GUYS!

Beneath it, Teddy had sent a selfie of himself wearing his school uniform, a maroon blazer and navy blue tie, making a twisted face like he'd just put a bag of Atomic Warheads in his mouth.

CAREFUL TEDDY, I typed, *I MIGHT MAKE THAT MY NEW PROFILE PIC.*

I clicked off my phone and slammed my locker door shut, securing it with the new sky-blue lock I'd convinced my mom to buy at Staples. As I rounded the corner, I heard a familiar voice heckling someone in the distance.

"Hey, watch where yer goin'," the voice bellowed. "Don't you know this is an eighth-grade hallway?"

"Oh, sorry," a wimpy voice responded.

"Yeah, I'm not sure if you know this, but we're upperclassmen now, which means you're on our turf."

The voice belonged to none other than my former bully turned castmate, Tanner Falzone. And while his words seemed strangely similar to lines from *West Side Story*, I decided to hang back.

"Uh, okay," the younger boy said, gripping the straps of his backpack and setting off.

"Wait a minute," Tanner barked, holding out his hand and pressing it against the kid's chest. "I'm not done with you. I'll let you go once you answer my question," he said, cocking his head. "Whose hallway is this?"

I couldn't help feeling bad for this little guy. I'd spent a whole semester terrified of Tanner, and even though I knew his bark was worse than his bite, I felt this underclassman's pain. I opened my mouth, ready to tell him to knock it off, when at that very second Lou and Jenny rounded the corner. In an instant, the tough look vanished from Tanner's face, and a twinkle gleamed in his eye.

"Yo, Benning," he called out, swaggering toward the pair. He reached out one of his meaty goalie legs and gave the side of her foot a little scuff.

"Nice choice on the kicks," he said, gesturing to her shoes. "Guess they had doll shoes after all." He laughed to himself, looking back and flashing a roguish grin.

Lou regained her footing and tried to keep walking, staring at the ground as her face turned beet red. The scrawny kid seized the opportunity and scurried off in the other direction, pleased with how quickly his troublesome bully had turned into a distracted flirt. I must have been enjoying the moment a little too much because Lou immediately threw me a nasty look.

"Well, I'm glad one thing hasn't changed over the summer," I said to Lou with a smirk. "Tanner Falzone obviously still has a crush on you."

"Ew, no he doesn't," Lou yipped.

"'Doll shoes,'" Jenny repeated. "What was he talking about?"

"Nothing!" Lou said, swatting her hands like she was trying to bat away a fruit fly. "I don't know. He's Tanner! He's always talking about something crazy."

I narrowed my eyes, sensing something fishy was going on. Maybe Lou didn't see it, but Tanner's focus had completely shifted the second she appeared.

"You know, speaking of crazy things, is it crazy to learn two parts?" Lou squeaked.

"Wait, what?" I asked.

"For *Sound of Music*!" she blurted out. "I worry that depending on who else auditions, I might be too short for Louisa or too tall for Brigitta. So I think I'm going to prepare both sides. That way I have a much better shot at getting cast if they skew tall."

I realized what was happening. Lou was a master at diverting attention away from anything that involved Tanner Falzone.

"Sure," I said reluctantly, giving in to Lou this round. "That sounds like a great idea."

☆ ☆ ☆ ☆ ☆

Back at home I slogged into my room, surprised by how exhausted and jarring my return to reality had been. First days of school were always cruel alarms, reminding you that summer vacation was officially over and you had 180 school days to go until the next one. I tossed my backpack into the corner and let my body fall face-first onto the bed. My nose was squished against the comforter, but I didn't move. It felt nice to not think about anything but the clean laundry smell and the faint sound of my dad unpacking groceries in the kitchen below.

Bzzz, the phone buzzed in my pocket.

I fished it out and rolled over onto my back, holding it above my head as I faced the ceiling.

Lou: *Hey Musketeers! How was everyone's first day?*

Bzzz

Kaylee: *Mine was alright. Like all my choir friends are in different classes this year. I can't with people who don't love singing.*

Bzzz

Louisa: *Boo :(I know how u feel. I'm just counting down the days until Jack and I can be in a musical again.*

Bzzz

KAYLEE: BTW MY HOMEWORK TONIGHT IS TO READ THE FIRST CHAPTER OF HUCK FINN. CAN I JUST LISTEN TO THE OVERTURE OF BIG RIVER INSTEAD?

Back and forth it went, Kaylee and Lou dissecting their classes, teachers, and friends' new hairstyles. Occasionally I'd chime in, but mostly I waited for Teddy to enter the conversation. After a particularly detailed account of Rustin Middle School's lunch menu, I decided it was time to take matters into my own hands.

I opened a new text message window, addressed not to the Four Musketeers, but to one person specifically.

WHAT ABOUT YOU, TEDDY? I began to write. *WE HAVEN'T HEARD ANYTHING ABOUT YOUR FIRST DAY.*

My fingers hesitated as I typed the next sentence. For some reason these three small words felt dangerous as they appeared on the screen.

I MISS YOU

My thumb hovered over the "send" button. *Should I send it or not?* I squinted my eyes and clenched my teeth. *It's just a text,* I said to myself.

For the past month, all the Four Musketeers had been doing was gush about how much we missed each other. This was hardly any different.

And yet . . .

But before I could hit *delete*, the weight of an invisible hand seemed to reach out and press down on my thumb.

Whoosh. Message sent.

Immediately I knew it was a mistake. I should have just said "we." "*We* miss you." My phone started feeling red-hot in my hand like the handle of a pot left on the stove for too long. I hurled it under my pillow; perhaps not being able to see it would help undo the last fifteen seconds.

Bzzz, the phone whispered, muffled from beneath the pillow.

Bzzz, it murmured again.

I looked around the room, not sure at who exactly; I was totally alone. I clenched my fist for a second before diving under the pillow, clasping onto the phone like a magic lamp.

"New Message from Teddy Waverly" a bubble on the screen announced.

This was a personal message, not one from the Four Musketeers.

Swipe, swipe, swipe, my fingers zipped across the screen.

AW THANKS FOR UR MESSAGE STINKER, his text read. *I MISS U2! WE SHOULD FACETIME.*

I could hardly believe it.

RIGHT NOW? I wrote back quickly.

Y NOT? he typed back.

My heart began to race. I dashed around my room, throwing clothes into the hamper and straightening papers on my desk. I ran over to the mirror and smoothed down my hair. Then messed it up. Then smoothed it down again. I bounced onto my bed, reached for my phone, and pressed the green "call" button. After waiting exactly five rings, a rectangle popped up, revealing a shiny black swath of hair and that one-in-a-million crooked smile that I would recognize even across the busiest intersection of Times Square.

"Jack!" He grinned into the phone camera.

"Hey, hey, hey," I replied, sounding more comedy-flyer-guy than intended.

"How ya been, skunk?" he asked.

"I've been great, how are you?"

"Pretty good."

Teddy was seated in a big chair with fancy

knobs carved out of wood at the top. Behind him was a gold-framed painting that looked like either a fox hunt or a cut scene from Sondheim's *A Little Night Music*.

"Are you in your . . . bedroom?" I asked.

"No"—he laughed—"I'm in my dad's study."

"Oh." I nodded.

I still hadn't gotten used to the contradiction that was Teddy Waverly. Upon first glance he seemed like such a proper, preppy rich kid, but once you got to know him he was a lot less Prince Eric and a lot more Pigpen from *Peanuts*.

"I'm supposed to be doing math homework," he continued, "Pythagorean theorem stuff, but I'm glad for the distraction."

As we swapped first-day-of-school stories, I realized we hadn't spoken since our awkward good-bye the last day of camp. Thankfully, we had fallen into our old routine, laughing and joking like we were back in cabin three, before everything had gotten . . . confusing.

"We had our first meeting for the Ghostlight competition today," Teddy said proudly.

Hearing the words *ghost* and *light*, I immediately sat up in my bed.

"Well, it wasn't really a meeting," he continued. "We actually have a class every day where we work on it."

"Oh right," I teased. *"Private school,"* I said in an affected accent.

Teddy stuck out his tongue.

"Yeah, they announced what show we're going to be using as our competition piece."

"Oh yeah, what is it?" I asked.

"How to Succeed in Business Without Really Trying."

"Such a good one!" I replied. "You're going to audition for J. Pierpont Finch, right? I mean, you're perfect for that part."

"Aw, thanks," Teddy said, crossing his eyes. "I guess so. I'm not sure they're going to take me seriously as the lead. But even if I got Bud Frump or Twimble, I would still be excited."

"You have a student director for the show, right?"

"Yeah, they announced that, too," Teddy said, his smile growing. "It's this girl named Wren."

"Wren?!" I squawked. "Like the bird?"

"Oh yeah." Teddy grinned. "Don't worry, she also has blue hair, so you *know* she's gonna do something kooky and inventive. Her dad is a theater professor at Northwestern and directs at Steppenwolf, this fancy theater company in Chicago."

"Yeah, I've heard of it." I nodded.

"I bet we do something crazy, like set the show in space or, like, Reno."

I was beginning to feel jealous again. Not only because Teddy and Kaylee were going to be hanging out in November but that his production of *How to Succeed* was beginning to sound a lot more interesting than the Shaker Heights Players' *Sound of Music*.

"Well, it sounds like a winning team," I said. "I'm sure Kaylee is already practicing her fake 'congratulations' speech for when you guys steal the trophy again."

"Stop." He rolled his eyes. "It's not about that. I know Kaylee jokes that all we care about is winning, but it's really about creating our own stuff without the help of adults. And, you know, getting to tell a story from our own point of view."

I could tell this wasn't just something a winner was taught to say to make his competition feel better. I was pretty sure he meant it. The more

Teddy talked about Ghostlight, the more envious I felt myself becoming. What originally seemed like an excuse to see a couple of my friends was starting to sound like something I would seriously regret missing out on.

"What if," I said, biting the corner of my lip, "what if *I* did the Ghostlight Festival?"

Teddy stared straight into the camera of his phone. For a moment he was silent, his expression hard to read.

"Don't mess with me, Jack Goodrich."

"Like, what if?" I shrugged.

"Do not get my hopes up if you are not serious."

"I don't know." I sighed. "It sounds fun. Although I guess it would be a lot to put together."

"Well, you would *have* to direct it," Teddy said. "Like, who knows more about Broadway stuff than Jack Goodrich? Look, Wren is cool and all, but she's not even close to being as big a nerd as you."

"Um. Thanks?" I raised an eyebrow.

"No, I just mean, you've had more experience than probably any eighth-grader who would compete in this thing. I'm sure you've worked with a lot of directors and seen what works and what doesn't. I bet you'd be a natural."

I could feel my mind swirling with thoughts. To be honest, I had no idea what our piece would look like, or what show we'd pick, or if we could even pull it off. But none of those things made me feel anxious. They made me feel exhilarated. I looked down at Teddy's face on my phone screen. Of course there was something else, too.

"Plus, I'd get to see you . . ." I stumbled, correcting myself . . . "*You guys*."

Teddy raised his eyebrows slightly.

"It would be just like camp again," I quickly added.

He looked away from the camera, perhaps at the clock on his dad's desk or the math homework that had gone untouched for the past forty-five minutes.

"What's Lou going to do?" Teddy asked.

I immediately felt a sinking feeling in my stomach. *Of course*. In all the excitement, I'd forgotten about my partner in crime. As far as Lou was concerned, I'd never even given the Ghostlight Festival a second thought. But shouldn't it count that I was *going to* bring it up with her? It's just that a poorly timed newspaper ad had stolen the spotlight.

"She'll probably still want to do *Sound of Music*. You have no idea how she gets when she's stuck on an idea."

"Well, that would suck." Teddy frowned. "You guys worked together so well on that song at camp. I can't imagine you doing it without her."

"Yeah," I murmured. "Me neither."

"Well, you should at least present her with the option," Teddy said after a pause. "Just tell her about it. You might be surprised. She might end up going for it. Plus, the actual competition is so fun! We basically take over a Marriott for three days. Like, everywhere you go it's theater kids in the elevator, theater kids in the pool, theater kids getting their arms stuck trying to steal a Twix bar from the vending machine . . ."

"How long were you stuck?" I deadpanned.

"Forty-five minutes, but that's beside the point," Teddy continued. "It's not just about people competing. It's about spending a weekend with kids who love musicals just as much as we do."

"Dinner's ready!" my dad's voice called up the stairway.

"Okay, I have to go," I said hurriedly. "Thanks for your advice—it was really great talking to you."

"You too, Jack Attack." He smiled. "Let me know what you end up choosing."

"I will. Break legs at auditions!"

Teddy beamed one last crooked smile into his phone and logged off. I couldn't figure out whether it was the rush of possibilities that came with directing my very own show or the fact that I'd finally gotten to talk with Teddy, but I bounced down the stairs with a huge grin on my face. I was going to make Ghostlight happen, I decided—I just needed to figure out how to get my best friend on board.

Louisa

"HEY, LOU—CAN WE TALK FOR a sec?"

It was the second day of school and Jack and I were walking from the bus to the main entrance, sidestepping clumps of middle-schoolers determined to enjoy every last minute of freedom before the first bell rang.

"Sure," I said, stopping in the middle of the walkway. "Is something wrong?"

I was instantly worried. What could have happened between yesterday and today that required a special before-school talk?

"Nothing's wrong," Jack assured me, shaking his

head for emphasis, "I just . . . have something I want to tell you."

I gripped the straps of my backpack, bracing myself. "What?"

Jack hesitated as if debating whether to continue.

"Well, I was FaceTiming with Teddy last night . . ."

He paused, and in that brief moment of silence between us I wondered with slight apprehension if my suspicions about Jack's feelings toward Teddy were about to be confirmed. I didn't know why it made me nervous to think about Jack possibly being gay. I mean, I found out Wayne Flanagan was gay toward the end of *Into the Woods* and it didn't change the way I thought about him at all. My mom's friend Kathryn had recently married a woman she'd been with for thirteen years and they had two kids, and it all seemed perfectly normal. Still, I just wasn't ready to talk about this stuff with my best friend. I wouldn't know what to say.

None of that mattered, though, because what Jack actually said next was:

"I don't think I want to audition for *Sound of Music*."

I was dumbfounded. Jack's statement came as such a surprise that I could only blink in response. Mostly because I was speechless, but also because I didn't want to start crying. Finally, after an awkward beat, I asked quietly, "Why not?"

"Well, because . . ." Jack looked down at his feet, shuffling them from side to side.

Because you're sick of me, I thought, my heart sinking, *because I've dragged you into every theatrical thing I could find since the moment you arrived in Shaker Heights and you could really use a break. Because you hate the Von Trapp family, because you're finally joining the soccer team, because—oh God!—you and your family are moving back to New York . . .*

"Because I think we should enter the Ghostlight Festival instead."

Okay, so maybe my first instinct was correct, and this *did* have something to do with Teddy? I'd personally forgotten all about the Ghostlight Festival, and with good reason.

"You want to do Ghostlight even though Teddy's school is basically guaranteed to win?"

He shrugged.

"It sounds fun."

"You want to enter a contest you know we won't win."

I eyed Jack skeptically, hearing Kaylee's laugh in my head as she teased Teddy about Cavendish's numerous victories.

"It's not all about winning," Jack said, and proceeded to tell me in animated detail about his conversation with Teddy the night before, about how Cavendish had decided to enter Ghostlight with a thirty-minute presentation of *How to Succeed in Business Without Really Trying*, how some girl named Wren (*Wren?*) was directing it, how MTNs got to take over a Marriott for a weekend . . . By the time he finished talking, it was clear that, whether he had a crush on Teddy or not, he was genuinely interested in entering the Ghostlight Festival.

"I think it could be a really cool experience," Jack concluded, searching my face to see if he'd convinced me in any way.

"Well," I began, still processing everything he'd said, "who would direct it? You?"

"That's what I was thinking," Jack said, cautiously, "which would also mean that I couldn't be in it."

"Why not?"

"It's part of the competition rules. Directors can't put themselves in their presentations." Jack must have known that this piece of information would make me even more skeptical, because he asked, almost apologetically, "Would you be okay with that?"

I didn't know how to answer because I didn't know if I was "okay" with *any* of this—five minutes earlier I'd been brainstorming ways to wear my hair for my *Sound of Music* audition. I flashed back to doing *Into the Woods* with Jack last fall, remembering how much fun we'd had with the Shaker Heights Players. *Sound of Music* was sure to be a blast, too, and even though I wasn't guaranteed a part, letting it go by without even trying felt like a huge sacrifice. On the other hand, a Marriott packed with MTNs sounded great, too, especially if it meant a Four Musketeers reunion. Rather than respond to Jack's question, I had one more of my own.

"What show would you want to do?"

"I don't know yet," Jack replied. "I was sort of hoping you'd help me decide." *Well, that's something,* I thought. It was always nice to be included in decision making, especially if it involved choosing a show. Even so, I wasn't ready to give in. Sensing this, Jack continued, "Listen, just think about it, okay? If you still want to do *Sound of Music*, I'll audition, too. I mean, there would be no point in doing Ghostlight without you." *Oh jeez*, I thought, *way to guilt-trip me, Jack!*

"Okay, I'll think about it." I nodded. The first bell rang.

"Thanks," Jack said, looking hopeful.

We let ourselves get swept up by the herd of kids making their way toward the school building, and I wondered how in the world I was going to be able to concentrate in any of my classes with so much to consider.

☆ ☆ ☆ ☆ ☆

By lunch I was no closer to making a decision and therefore had no appetite, choosing to head to the library instead of braving the chaos of the cafeteria. *What should I do?* I kept asking myself as I wandered down one of the empty hallways, when suddenly, as if in answer to my question, a redheaded fireball emerged from the teacher's lounge down the hall, calling over her shoulder to someone inside, "See you later, hon!"

"Belinda!" I shouted, prompting the one and

only Belinda Grier to pivot in my direction, landing in a perfect third position. Though she had been living in Shaker Heights since January, she still looked like she'd just stepped out of a New York dance studio. A long knitted maroon tunic draped off her shoulder, while zebra-print tights continued their safari into ankle-high black suede booties.

"Well, if it isn't Louisa 'Lou' Benning!" she shouted back, then thrust out her arms like Mama Rose, inviting me in for a hug. I ran and flung my arms around her—my fairy godmother, here to rescue me.

"Wow," she said, holding me out at arm's length and studying my face, "you are getting *pretty*."

I wasn't used to being called pretty. Jenny was pretty, especially now that she looked like a grown-up, but I didn't think I was. *Cute* and *adorable* were the words people used to describe my appearance, usually by my parents' friends or by the receptionist at the dentist's office. The word *pretty* seemed utterly foreign, so of course I blushed, embarrassed. Belinda laughed.

"I'm *serious*, Miss Thing," she said. "You're going to start breaking some hearts pretty soon."

An image of Tanner grinning at me by our

lockers the day before flashed across my mind, making my palms start to sweat. Instantly uncomfortable, I quickly changed the subject.

"What are you doing here?" I asked. Belinda had filled in to direct our production of *Guys and Dolls* last spring after our music teacher, Mrs. Wagner, was injured in a skiing accident in Colorado. She also substitute taught occasionally, but it seemed unlikely that she'd be doing so on the second day of school. And because of this, it was Belinda's turn to blush.

"I, um," she began, then pursed her lips together to suppress a giggle, "I was bringing Coach Wilson his lunch." We shared a knowing smile as I thought back to how excited Coach Wilson was when Belinda returned home to Shaker Heights. They had performed opposite each other in their high-school production of *Once Upon a Mattress*, many years ago. Looked like Princess Winnifred and Prince Dauntless were now romantically linked offstage, as well.

"What are *you* doing?" Belinda asked, looking around the deserted hallway. "Shouldn't you be in the cafeteria?"

I sighed heavily and gave her a pathetic look.

"Oh, child," she said, putting her arm around me, "I know sighs like that. Come with me and let's chat it out."

You might think that a big empty theater feels lonely, but sitting on the edge of the stage with Belinda Grier during my lunch period was the coziest situation I could have imagined. It was so strange to think that only months before, she and I had squared off in this very place during an incredibly tense rehearsal for *Guys and Dolls*. But a lot had changed since then, and right now I really needed her help.

"That *is* a conundrum," Belinda conceded after I'd explained to her my *Sound of Music* vs. Ghostlight dilemma, "but Jack has said he'll do whatever you decide?"

I nodded, feeling a little queasy. Belinda smiled.

"Gosh—isn't it terrible having kind and decent friends?"

"It *is*!" I lamented, dropping my head into my hands. The fact that Jack was being so generous really did make this whole thing much harder.

"Here's the thing, darling," Belinda said, gently

patting my back, "what you have here is known as a *champagne problem*."

I sat up and looked at her.

"Huh?"

"This may seem like a tough decision, but really—you get to choose between two favorable outcomes. No matter what, you'll have a great experience with your best friend by your side. I mean, if you choose *Sound of Music*, you'll both still have to get cast, but please . . . we all know you two have a pretty good shot at that, right?"

"Right," I said quietly, not wanting to appear presumptuous.

"And Jack has made you a *direct offer* to be in his Ghostlight show, which—*come on*—is the best thing you can hope for in show business. So before you start feeling too sorry for yourself, hon, just remember that there are much harder things to choose between," she said pointedly, then straightened out her tights so the zebra stripes looked more stripy and less wavy. *Like choosing between staying in New York City or moving back to Shaker Heights, Ohio?* I wondered, thinking back to how difficult it must have been for Belinda to give up her dreams of being a Broadway star. I stared out at the vacant rows of seats, seeking answers from an invisible audience. I could feel myself leaning in a certain direction as I pictured a hotel full of kids, all singing and dancing in shows that they had put together themselves. But I was still hung up on one thing.

"Ghostlight just seems like a lot of work for nothing!" I blurted out. How was entering an unwinnable contest a "favorable outcome"?

"Because of this other school? This school where your camp friend goes?" Belinda asked.

"Yeah, Cavendish. They've won for the last eleven years." I sighed, already feeling defeated. Belinda suddenly grabbed my shoulders and turned me to face her. I could smell her perfume, exotic and smoky.

"Hey," she said forcefully, fixing me with her green-eyed stare, "what kind of attitude is this? When did you get so pessimistic?"

I gulped. She made a good point.

"It's one thing if you'd rather do the Players' show; fine. But if Ghostlight is something you *want* to do, then you're not doing it 'for nothing.' Don't let some other school's track record get in the way of that."

She let go of my shoulders, smoothed out her tunic, and checked her watch, making me think that my session with Dr. Belinda was over. But then she said one more thing, which would ultimately turn my champagne problem into a champagne solution.

"And don't sell yourself short, kiddo. Maybe Cavendish has won this Ghostlight thing for the past eleven years—but they've never gone up against Jack Goodrich and Louisa Benning."

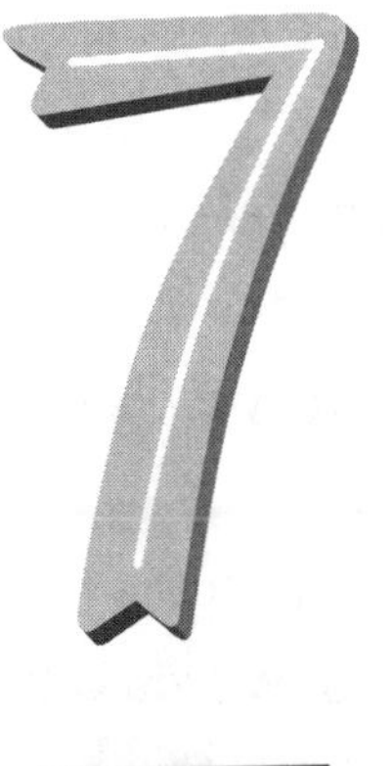

Jack

"So, I've given it some thought," Lou said the next day in gym class as we waited on the sidelines for our turn at kickball.

"Oh yeah?" I asked, bracing myself for Lou to pop my Ghostlight dreams like a chewing gum bubble.

"This Ghostlight thing sounds like it could be a lot of fun, but . . ."

My heart instantly sank. *So much for the Four Musketeers,* I thought. *So much for herds of MTNs singing Disney medleys.*

So much for getting to see Teddy again.

"But," she said, gathering her thoughts, "I've had

my heart set on *Sound of Music* for so long, y'know?"

"Totally," I said, my fingernails digging into the grooves of the metal bench. *Just say it, Lou. Say you'd rather be singing "So Long, Farewell" than road-tripping to a hotel with your best friend for a Camp Curtain Up reunion.*

"So after giving it a lot of thought—"

"Benning," Coach Wilson called, looking up from his clipboard. "You're up!"

"So after giving it a lot of thought . . . ?" I pleaded.

"One sec, I gotta kick!" she said, lazily skipping to home plate.

I almost rolled off the bench onto the dusty floor of the dugout.

"Lou, you're killing me!"

"Don't worry," she whispered. "I'll get out, like, immediately."

Lou sidled up to home plate looking about as uncomfortable as Coach Wilson would have been standing at a ballet barre. Sebastian Maroney, wearing a smirk you could see all the way from the pitcher's mound, launched his first pitch straight at Lou, who halfheartedly stuck out her leg, making just enough contact to roll the ball straight back into Sebastian's hands.

Like I said, gym class isn't exactly our forte.

"Oh, come on, Lou. You didn't even try!" Coach Wilson shouted from the sidelines as Lou trotted back to the bench.

"So . . . ?" I asked, practically jumping out of my skin.

Lou took a seat, crossed her arms, and winked at me.

"I'm in."

I had to cover my mouth so I wouldn't squeal with joy (gym class had proven to be a good thing today, but I wasn't about to press my luck).

"But," she added rigidly, "I want us to win."

"Oh . . . kay."

"Admit it: You're just as sick as I am of hearing about how Teddy's snooty school gets the trophy handed to them every year like they're Audra-freaking-McDonald," she said. "If I'm giving up *Sound of Music*, it's not for a participation medal."

I nodded, slowly realizing that the obsession Lou normally reserved for perfecting our auditions may have just found a new outlet.

"I already have a great idea for the show," she said, flashing a grin. "What about *The Fantasticks*?"

☆ ☆ ☆ ☆ ☆

As soon as Lou said it, I knew it was the perfect choice. *The Fantasticks* was a jewel box of a musical that had been running for more than fifty years off-Broadway. It tells the story of Matt and Luisa, two next-door neighbors whose fathers have built a wall to keep them from ever seeing each other, but despite their parents' warnings, the two fall madly in love. Meanwhile, the fathers are secretly best friends and have built the wall knowing that their children will, of course, disobey them.

My mom and dad had taken me to see the *The Fantasticks* back when we lived in New York, and I'd fallen completely in love with it. The musical was simply staged on a shoestring budget, with almost no set—just a sheet, a trunk, and a few props—yet the show still felt magical. After eight shows a week performing in *Mary Poppins*, where nannies flew, statues came to life, and chimney sweeps tap-danced on the ceiling, I was amazed to see how much of a spectacle you could put on with just a handful of actors, a couple of pieces of fabric, and an irresistible melody.

☆☆☆☆☆

"So, Jack, what do you think?" Lou said, snapping me back to reality.

"I . . . I think it's a great idea!"

"And don't you think I'd make a great Luisa?" she said, batting her eyelids.

"You don't just want to do it because you'd get to play a character with the same name as you, right?" I joked.

"Um, there's a Louisa in *Sound of Music*, too," Lou said. "My name is *very* prevalent in musical theater, Jack. And if I recall correctly, a certain someone was pretty desperate to nail his solo as Jack in *Into the Woods . . .*"

"Fair enough," I said, rolling my eyes. "All right, so we're doing *The Fantasticks*."

Saying it out loud made me laugh a little bit. I wasn't sure how in the world we were going to pull it off, but just speaking the words meant it had to be a little bit true.

"So, where do we start?" I asked.

"Oh." Lou reached slyly into the pocket of her sweatpants and pulled out a little piece of paper. "I thought you'd never ask."

☆ ☆ ☆ ☆ ☆

The next week felt like a spy movie with the two of us cast as secret agents assigned to Operation: Assemble Team *Fantasticks*. Once again, I came to realize how lucky I was to have a partner as capable as Lou. If Agent Goodrich was the one to hatch a plan, Agent Benning was the one to execute it. But producing a musical of our own would take more than just flyers, mass texts, and notes stuffed in lockers.

"The first thing on our checklist," Lou said, reading off the piece of paper I'd dubbed her Master Plan, "is 'Get a Choreographer.' I figure whoever we ask can also double as the Mute, since that character does the bulk of dancing in the show."

Jenny was the obvious choice, of course, but since her recent brush with professional dance over the summer, she'd become blasé about anything as juvenile as a middle-school theatrical production.

"I'm already bored with eighth grade," Jenny had groaned on our first day of school. "I wish we could just skip it and go right into high school."

She certainly looked ready for high school, not to mention that she'd begun dabbling in the world of eyeliner. Still, Lou wondered if choreographing a show might just be the pickup Jenny needed.

We met her at her locker right as the final school bell rang.

"Well, it depends," Jenny said, tugging on her jacket. "Are you thinking the choreography would be in the *Vaganova* or *Cecchetti* method of ballet? I can do either, obvi, but it'd be good to know what you had in mind before I signed on."

"I was thinking more in the musical staging . . . method," I said, squeezing the straps of my backpack. "We're just doing a thirty-minute version, so there's really not a ton of dancing, more just stylized movement.

"Huh," Jenny said, slamming her locker shut. "So *Cecchetti* is out."

"Probably." Lou clenched her teeth. "But there's a number where it rains, so maybe *confetti* is in."

Jenny nodded slowly, looking back and forth between Lou and me.

"Well . . . even Martha Graham had to keep it simple now and then," she said finally. "I'll do it."

Next on Lou's Master Plan: "Find an Adult Supervisor."

Of course there was only one choice. The theater gods must have been smiling on us, because when we arrived at music class the following morning we were greeted not by Mrs. Wagner, but by our old director Belinda Grier (dressed in a long-sleeve red leotard and skirt that could have easily been a repurposed Cassie costume from *A Chorus Line*).

"Mrs. Wagner is out with the flu, poor thing," Belinda announced to the class. "You'd think spending half a year in a body cast was bad enough, but hey, what do I know?" she said out of the corner of her mouth. "Anyway, she didn't leave me any lesson plans, so I guess I'll just do what I do best—improvise!"

For Belinda, "improvising" meant dishing stories about a nightmare summer-stock experience in Sioux Falls, South Dakota.

"And that's why you should always get your agent to negotiate your housing," she announced to the classroom. "Or you just might end up sleeping in a room decorated with a hundred antique dolls."

The second the bell rang, we hurried to her desk to tell her our decision.

"I'm so glad you went with Ghostlight," she said, taking a swig from her Broadway Dance Center water bottle. "I think this is going to be really good for you two."

"I think so, too," I said, beaming.

"I remember auditioning for Luisa right when I moved to New York," Belinda said, staring off into the middle distance dreamily. "I lived off of egg noodles for a week so I could save up to buy this perfect little white lace dress for the audition."

"How did it go?" Lou asked.

"Oh," Belinda said, tossing the bottle into her bedazzled duffel bag. "I think my feedback was that I was too *energetic*. You know, it's hard to contain all of *this* in a hundred-seat theater," she said, drawing a big circle around her face with her finger. "I'm really more primed for a Broadway house, anyway."

We nodded in solemn agreement.

"About that competition, though." She smiled. "Of course I'll be your supervisor."

☆ ☆ ☆ ☆ ☆

"Next in the Master Plan," Lou read from the list as we walked to science class, "is casting."

"Well, you're obviously playing Luisa," I said, pulling a pencil out of my pocket and scribbling her name next to the character. "But who do we get to play the other lead? Matt?"

"Are you sure *you* can't be it?" Lou whined.

"Not if I'm going to direct." I shrugged. "That's the rule."

Plus, I was excited about the prospect of running the show. There were always going to be things for us to audition for, but how often did someone our age get to call the shots?

As Lou and I rounded the corner back to our lockers, we passed the school's impossibly huge trophy case. A framed picture of last year's boys' soccer team hung front and center, their bright red jerseys peeking from behind a row of gold-painted trophies. Lou practically screeched to a halt, her eyes trained on number 1.

"I know what you're thinking, Lou," I said, following her gaze. "But their season is about to go into full swing."

"No, I know," she grumbled. "But how good would Sebastian Maroney be as Matt? Look at what he did with Sky Masterson."

"Yeah, he'd be perfect," I admitted. "But he's the captain of the team! They practice, like, every day. There's no way he'd have time to rehearse."

"Fine," Lou huffed. "Well, who were you thinking to play El Gallo, then?"

El Gallo was the narrator of the show who gets hired by the two fathers to kidnap Luisa (another ploy to get Matt to heroically rescue her and fall even deeper in love). This needed to be a guy with a rich deep voice and the presence of someone older and mischievous.

"What about William Kerrigan-Hyde?" Lou suggested.

"Scrawny little William Kerrigan-Hyde who played Nicely-Nicely Johnson?"

"Nooo," Lou said, raising her eyebrows. "I mean big, tall William Kerrigan-Hyde whose voice changed and who went through a giant growth spurt over the summer. He *used* to be a high tenor, but now I bet he'd sound great singing a baritone standard like 'Try to Remember.'"

William's eyes lit up in science class when we suggested having him play a character with a dark, mysterious side.

"It sounds like a fun role. And if you'd like," he said, running a finger across his upper lip, "I could even grow out my mustache."

We squinted, studying his face, but there only

seemed to be a whisper of peach fuzz below his nose.

"Sure." Lou nodded. "If you think it would help."

"Oh, it would," William, said nodding his head. "It definitely would."

☆ ☆ ☆ ☆ ☆

"How are we going to find boys to play the fathers?" Lou asked, reading the next two roles off her checklist, Hucklebee and Bellomy.

I was ready for this question. After our difficulty finding boys for *Guys and Dolls*, I knew we'd have to think outside the box to cast *The Fantasticks*. Most of the roles in the show were for male actors, and this time there wouldn't be a soccer team with an off-season to swoop in and save the day.

"What if they were mothers?" I suggested. "We're supposed to write our own adaptation of the show. I don't think it changes anything if they're played by girls. In fact, we get judged on creativity, so it might even work in our favor."

"Look at you," Lou teased. "You're acting like a director already."

Esther Blick and Sarah Fineberg were our first and only asks. They played Agatha and General Cartwright from the Save-a-Soul Mission in *Guys and Dolls*. Both had natural comic timing and were eager to sink their teeth into leading roles, even if it meant playing characters three times their age.

☆☆☆☆☆

We didn't even have to brainstorm actors to play Henry and Mortimer, the pair of old Shakespearean actors who assist El Gallo in the kidnapping scene, because Belinda delivered them right to our lunch table.

"I'd like you to meet Raj and Radhika Jupti," she said, placing her hands on the shoulders of two strikingly similar kids.

"They're seventh-graders who just transferred this year," Belinda said. "Brother-and-sister twins all the way from jolly old England."

The boy had a messy pile of black hair, and the girl, two long plaited pigtails. Both wore identical smiles.

"I had them in my morning class and we got to chatting," Belinda continued. "You'll never believe what show they performed in their boarding school last year."

Raj took a step forward, blushing slightly. "William Shakespeare's *Twelfth Night*."

"We played Sebastian and Viola," the girl said. "Naturally."

The last period of the day was study hour, and for the first time in a week I found myself alone, staring at the final entry on our checklist: the role of Matt.

WHERE R U? I texted Lou, sneaking my phone out from its hiding place beneath the flap of my flannel shirt. ***SHE'S ABOUT TO TAKE ATTENDANCE AND UR STILL NOT HERE.***

"Abigail Abbott," our librarian, Mrs. Westphal, called out.

"Here!"

"Zachary Avalon."

"Present!"

"Louisa Benning," Mrs. Westphal read.

I stared at the entrance to the library. *C'mon, Lou.*

"Louisa?" Mrs. Westphal looked around the room. "Is Louisa Benning here?"

"I'm here!" shouted Lou, busting through the door, a crumpled sheet of paper held aloft triumphantly. She looked disheveled but delighted to be there.

"Where were you?" I whispered as she collapsed into the chair next to me.

"Just doing a little last-minute detective work," she panted, sliding the mystery piece of paper across the table.

I flipped it over and began reading what seemed to be a schedule filled in with dates and names.

"What is this?"

"It's the entire practice and game schedule for the soccer team for the next two months," Lou wheezed. "I stole it off of Coach Wilson's desk."

"You did WHAT?!" I said, completely ignoring the "Silence Is Golden" poster on the wall to my left. I knew when Lou put her mind to something, she went all in, but I never presumed it would involve a rendezvous with crime.

"Okay, not exactly," Lou hushed me. "I sort of got Belinda to steal it and xerox me a copy, but it was totally *my* idea."

"What do you need this for?!"

"Well, look," Lou said, pointing to the calendar at the bottom of the page. "Notice anything missing?"

I scanned the dates and numbers, but nothing

seemed to be jumping out as very "clue-worthy."

"Not really. There's practice every day of the week, just like we guessed," I said, pushing it back across the table.

"Right," Lou said, "but on Tuesdays and Thursdays it's only the *girls'* soccer team that's called for practice. Plus, on the weeks where they play a game at home, they get Sundays off."

I stared at the sheet again. "So what you're saying is—"

"—maybe there's a way to convince Sebastian Maroney to rehearse with us on those days," Lou said, finishing my thought.

Like an actor being fed his cue line, a voice piped up from behind us.

"What *about* Sebastian Maroney?"

We spun around in our chairs to find the man of the hour standing above us carrying a stack of books, looking like a typical eighth-grade boy, not at all like the hero who'd shown up in the last ten minutes of our spy movie to possibly crack the case.

"He-eyy, Sebastian," Lou said, tilting her head. "Sooo, remember when you helped the soccer team win those big games last year?"

"Yeah," Sebastian replied. "We were district champs."

"Right, right." Lou nodded. "Well, this year, how'dja like to win an even *bigger* trophy?"

☆ ☆ ☆ ☆ ☆

I'll never forget walking into the Shaker Heights Middle School auditorium that first Sunday. I'd been to a lot of first rehearsals, and they always brought about the same fun rituals—highlighting lines in your script, announcing the role you'd be playing, feeling that rush when it was your first time speaking as a new character—but they were nothing compared to this. We were back in the auditorium where I'd spent so many hours rehearsing, but today I was wearing a different hat. I walked down the aisle and took my position at the front of the room, looking out at the cast we'd spent days assembling.

In their faces I saw the afternoon we'd spent begging Principal Lang to make Team Ghostlight an official club so we could get school funding. I could still smell the printer toner from when Belinda ran off copies of the permissions slip she'd drawn up for us. I could hear my mom's voice echoing through the living room as she went down the cast list, calling every parent to see if they could join her as a chaperone for the Ghostlight weekend. I saw the stacks of binders and punched holes of script pages scattered across my bedroom carpeting like snowflakes.

"Good morning," I said in a loud, clear voice. "Thank you so much for joining us today to work on *The Fantasticks*—Tom Jones and Harvey Schmidt's classic musical."

I looked around the room at Lou and Sebastian, perched in the center, their scripts open and lines already highlighted. At Jenny by their side, armed with a pen and big pink binder with the words *Dance Bible* splashed across it. At William and Raj and Radhika, Sarah and Esther, all of them looking to me for answers and trusting that whatever decisions I'd make were for the sake of the show. I glanced over to Belinda, armed with a notepad and pen with a silver tinsel pom-pom on the end. She nodded for me to continue.

"You know," I said, "*The Fantasticks* is the longest-running show to have ever appeared in New York. Its first production off-Broadway ran for forty-two years. Unfortunately, we don't have *quite* that much time," I added. "Only eight weeks, so I guess we should dive right in and begin reading through the script."

I took a seat in the folding chair and opened my binder.

"Skip the pages I crossed out. Those are cut for time. And, oh," I said, another thought popping into my head. "I guess I should maybe read the stage directions."

"Oh no, honey," Belinda piped up from her seat. "Let me. You shouldn't have to do anything but listen and give it your full attention." She smiled and gave me a wink. "You're the director now."

And with that, I leaned back in my chair and closed my eyes. As she spoke, my brain began firing and flashing with images. All that worry that I'd mess things up or not have enough good ideas seemed to fall away, and the prospect of coming up with something new, something maybe even great was enough to let me know I was in the right place.

"*This play should be played on a platform,*" she read. "*There is no scenery, but occasionally a stick may be held up to represent a wall. Or a cardboard moon may be hung upon a pole to indicate that it is night.*"

Louisa

TWO WEEKS AFTER OUR FIRST rehearsal I couldn't believe how quickly the time was flying. Neither could my camp friends, who, upon learning that Jack and I had signed up for Ghostlight, had practically lost their minds with excitement and were now counting down the days until our reunion.

Wistful camp memories had been replaced with plans for our Marriott takeover, while jokes about—well, everything—flooded my phone with buzzes and chirps throughout each day. The biggest news—that Kaylee had been cast in the lead role of Ti Moune in her school's presentation of

Once on This Island, had prompted a new tradition that Kaylee liked to call "Role Call," in which we all had to announce our characters' names at the beginning of our respective rehearsals. So on Tuesday afternoon of our third week of rehearsals, as I sat in the auditorium waiting for Jack to announce his game plan for the afternoon, I decided to take the initiative and get our "role call" started.

ME: *ROLE CALL! LUISA PRESENT! (AND SO IS JACK—BUT HE IS BUSY GETTING READY TO DIRECT!!)*

KAYLEE: *TI MOUNE IN THE HOUSE!*

TEDDY: *J. PIERPONT FINCH REPORTING 4 DUTY!*

KAYLEE: *ONLY 4 WEEKS TIL WE'RE ALL TOGETHER!!!*

TEDDY: *WOOT WOOT!*

"Looks like somebody's in a good mood."

Startled, I looked up to see Belinda standing over me, an amused expression on her face.

"Oh! I was just texting with our friends from camp," I explained, blushing slightly. "They're both gonna be at Ghostlight, too."

"Of course, the perennial winners," Belinda said, her faux leather stretch pants making a sticky rubbery sound against the worn wood of the chair as she squeezed into the seat next to mine.

"Well, only one trophy goes to the winning school, actually," I explained. "My friend Kaylee's school has never even placed. But she just got cast as Ti Moune in their presentation of *Once on This Island*, so she's super psyched."

"As she should be," Belinda said. "I saw the original production of it in New York—and I'm talking the original *off*-Broadway production, before it moved to Broadway—and it was *stunning*. Your friend must be pretty talented if she's playing Ti Moune."

"Oh, she's incredible," I said, thinking back to Kaylee's performance at our camp revue. "I can't wait for you to meet her."

"So, you feeling good about your decision?" Belinda asked, making a sweeping gesture across the auditorium. The sleeve of her leopard-print blouse slid down her arm, revealing about a dozen sparkly bracelets. (I wondered how much closet space Belinda had, since I'd never seen her wear the same thing twice.)

"Totally," I replied, taking in the scene. "This is really cool."

I'd never been a part of something that was almost entirely done by kids. You might think that putting us in charge of something would be a recipe for disaster—lots of goofing off and not taking things seriously—but you'd be wrong. It was, in fact, pretty much the opposite of those things; we were even more serious about our work because it was all ours.

In one corner sat Sebastian and William, each with a set of earbuds tucked snugly in their ears, their musical scores laid out in front of them as they quietly sang along with the accompaniment that Mr. Hennessy had recorded for them. I laughed silently as I watched William carefully stroking his upper lip. Having claimed to be able to grow a mustache after getting cast as El Gallo, he'd become obsessed with its growth and had therefore developed this hilarious habit, coaxing the hair follicles to deliver what was (in his opinion) the defining feature of his character. I clearly wasn't the only one to notice, because all of a sudden I heard Belinda's voice whispering in my ear:

"I hope William knows that a full mustache doesn't translate to a full performance." And with that my silent laugh became a full-on giggle.

Meanwhile, in another corner, Raj and Radhika Jupti were busy coming up with their comedic bits for Henry and Mortimer, the aging (and often forgetful) actor and his oddball sidekick. In the original script, it says that Mortimer is dressed as an American Indian, but Raj and Radhika, of course, were originally from India, so they suggested we dispense with the headdresses and war paint and instead embrace their cultural heritage, which we all thought was a great idea.

"I can borrow one of my mother's saris," Radhika had announced, "though I will need a lot of safety pins; they are all very long."

Finally, onstage, Jack and Jenny were working with Sarah and Esther on their duet, "Never Say No," in which the two fathers (now mothers) explain their theory: that the best way to get your children to do something is to tell them *not* to do it:

"And children, I guess, must get their own way
The minute that you say no."

Jenny, who had prepared for her role as choreographer by cramming YouTube videos of famous dance routines set by legendary choreographers Jerome Robbins, Michael Kidd, and Agnes de Mille (all former ballet dancers, of course), had quickly come to the realization that her newfound knowledge of musical theater dance history would be of little use to Sarah and Esther, who were both woefully lacking in coordination. But what they lacked in physical grace was definitely made up for in comedic timing, so Jack and Jenny had decided to take a more slapstick approach to the number. Instead of pivot turns and jazz squares, Sarah and Esther were bumping into each other and tripping over benches like they were in an old vaudeville comedy routine. It was great.

"Smart," Belinda murmured, watching my friends turn lemons into lemonade. "That's not an easy skill—being able to adapt to the circumstances you're given—but Jack and Jenny are doing it naturally." I turned to see that she was genuinely impressed.

"You know," she said, and I could tell a Belinda zinger was on its way, "there are a couple Broadway directors and choreographers I'd like to invite down here. Maybe they could learn a thing or two."

As I looked around the auditorium, I felt awash with pride knowing that I'd helped to assemble this impressive group. Even though I wasn't the director, I still felt a certain kind of ownership of the project, and it made me excited in a new way—a way I never would have felt if I'd been cast in *The Sound of Music.*

"Hey, Jack?" Belinda's voice suddenly cut through the room, seizing Jack's attention.

"Yes?" he asked, peering out toward our row. Belinda consulted her watch, its rhinestone border catching the light.

"You said you wanted to move on to 'Metaphor' by 3:30, and it's 3:35."

"Yeah, that's right. Thanks," said Jack, clapping his hands together. "Sarah, Esther, and Jenny—you cool to keep working on stuff in the back of the auditorium?"

"Totally," said Jenny, grabbing her water bottle from the edge of the stage. "C'mon, girls." They all hopped onto the floor as Jack called out, "Sebastian and Lou—you ready?"

Am I ever, I thought, scooting past Belinda and bounding down the aisle, happy as I could possibly be.

☆ ☆ ☆ ☆ ☆

Oh, but all that pride, excitement, and happiness came to a screeching halt the next day.

"William just quit the show."

Jenny and I were on our way to French class when Jack intercepted us in a wide-eyed panic.

"What?" I gasped, having of course heard what he'd said but refusing to believe it. The image of him with his earbuds, mouthing the words to his songs, suddenly took on an utterly tragic hue. Speaking of hues, Jack looked positively green.

"He got his first grade on a math test yesterday and it was below a ninety."

"So?"

"I'm sorry, did you say below a *ninety*?" Jenny asked, incredulous.

"Yes."

"How far below a ninety?"

"I don't know! It doesn't matter!" Jack spat out, clearly distraught. "His parents are super strict, and they blame our show for being too much of a 'distraction.' So they're making him quit."

"Are you sure he's not just chickening out because he can't actually grow a mustache?" Jenny asked.

"This is no time for jokes!" Jack wailed.

"I'm being serious!" Jenny shouted back.

"Hold on—why doesn't he just promise to study harder?" I asked in desperation. "I mean, it seems like his parents are kind of overreacting, right? Over one test?"

"Doesn't matter," Jack said, shaking his head woefully, "they won't let him do it. He's out."

We all groaned in shared misery.

"Ugh! Who are we going to find to replace him?" Jack lamented, searching our faces for answers. Just then the bell rang.

"Shoot, we gotta run or we'll be late," I said, feeling guilty for having to leave Jack alone in his despair.

"We'll figure something out," Jenny called over her shoulder as we jogged down the hall. I found myself grimly wishing that I could share her confidence. It wasn't like El Gallos grew on trees around here.

☆ ☆ ☆ ☆ ☆

"Je voudrais un billet a Paris."

The last thing I wanted was to be partnered with Tanner Falzone in French class. But here we were, sitting on opposite sides of his desk, having been randomly assigned by Monsieur Radnor to act out an exchange between a passenger and ticket agent in some French train station. All around us our classmates garbled French words to one another in self-conscious monotones.

"Aller-simple ou aller-retour?"

I myself was a very distracted ticket agent. Unfortunately, my customer noticed.

"What's your deal, Benning?" Tanner, breaking character, was looking for any excuse not to speak French. It was understandable, since his accent left much to be desired. I shook my head, offering up a French word that I actually knew by heart.

"Rien."

"Huh?"

"Nothing," I said, fiddling with my pen.

"Fine. Don't tell me. Just don't make me say any more lame French things."

Pas de problème, I thought, further indulging in bilingual self-pity.

"Seriously, what's up?" Tanner asked. For some reason he didn't want to let me off the hook. "Did you sing a wrong note or something?"

I grimaced. Tanner was always so pleased with himself when he made jokes like that, no matter how stupid they were. But then came the Grin. I wanted to smack it off his face, but also . . . not. I looked over at Monsieur Radnor, who was completely engrossed in his Kindle. Assured that we were safe from reprimand, I sighed and reluctantly began to talk, keeping my voice low so as not to attract attention.

"You know that thing we're doing? The thing Sebastian's doing? With us?"

"Oh yeah, that play contest thing?"

"Yeah, well, we just lost one of our most important guys."

"Who?"

"William Hyde."

"How come?"

"Strict parents."

"Bummer."

I couldn't tell if Tanner was actually interested in any of this or just bored enough to carry on a conversation with me about my problems. I hesitated, waiting for him to become more interested in something else—like, say, the etched grooves on his desk, or the mark on the floor where a chair leg had scraped, or the sound of his own breathing. But he didn't; he just kept his eyes fixed on me.

"Yeah, total bummer," I said finally, averting my gaze. Tanner pressed on.

"So do you guys, like, have to drop out of the contest now?"

"I don't know—hopefully not."

"What part was William supposed to play?"

"El Gallo."

"Who's that?"

Still not convinced that Tanner cared about any of this, I cautiously began to describe the role: a tall and commanding figure who needed to be sort of menacing yet really charming; slightly cruel yet also sensitive.

"Huh," Tanner said when I finished my description. "Well. Good luck finding somebody."

He looked down at his French workbook as Monsieur Radnor's voice cut through the room.

"*Mademoiselles et Monsieurs*, it is time to switch roles, *s'il vous plaît*. The *passager* becomes the *agent de la billetterie*, and vice versa."

I sighed again as I turned back the page of my workbook to where we'd started our French scene, then looked up with a start as I realized Tanner had suddenly leaned across the desk so that his face was very close to mine. I felt my heartbeat quicken as I realized I wanted to simultaneously run out of the room and—yikes—lean in even closer. "Tanner, what are you—"

"*Oh la la*," he interrupted, whispering in a ridiculous French accent, "I've always wanted to play the *agent de* blah de blah."

Even though I was still upset about William dropping out, and even though the fate of our Ghostlight participation was now a complete unknown, I couldn't help it—I laughed. Loud enough that I had to cover my mouth with my hand so that Monsieur Radnor wouldn't know it was me. Triumphant, Tanner just leaned back in his seat and shook his head at me, his lips curling in a devilish smile.

"Benning," he chided under his breath, "I'm just trying to sell you a train ticket. Don't get me in trouble." And it was in that moment that I saw very clearly: a tall and commanding, sort of menacing yet really charming, slightly cruel yet also sensitive person sitting right across from me.

Jack

"TANNER FALZONE?!" I BLURTED into the phone. Even saying the name out loud made me shudder. He was the last, the *very* last person I expected Lou to offer up as a potential El Gallo. "Why, because you like him now?"

"Ew, no!" she yipped into my ear with a disgust so piercing that I had to pull the phone away from my head. "No, it's nothing like that. We're desperate," she whined. "You said so yourself."

"Apparently!" I hooted. "I guess I didn't realize just *how* desperate."

"I'm serious, Jack." I could hear Lou's voice tensing. "El Gallo is supposed to be tall, slick, and menacing. Tanner is *nothing* if not menacing. It was so clear in French class today. Plus, Sebastian already promised it's okay to miss the game the weekend of the competition. They're playing Adlai Stevenson, and we beat them last year thirteen to nothing."

The phone was beginning to feel hot against my cheek. I thought back to my first semester at SHMS, back when I lived in fear of ever coming in contact with the huge, blustering seventh-grader that was Tanner Falzone. Even after he surprised us and joined the cast of *Guys and Dolls* in the role of Big Jule, he still made me suspicious. That being said, he *was* pretty funny onstage and *was* awfully convincing with his tough-guy act, but this was way different. El Gallo was a much bigger part—and one that required a good deal of singing.

"I've gone through everybody else in our grade," Lou said. "Trust me, I'd never suggest him if I thought even one other person could do it. And besides, do we want to win or not?"

I did want to win. Even though it didn't seem like a big deal at the beginning, once I started seeing how good our show was, I couldn't help daydreaming about the awards ceremony, running up onto the stage and feeling the weight of the trophy in my hands.

"All right. Let's call him." I sighed. "But you have to do it. If I call Tanner Falzone and ask him to give up his free time, free time that I'm sure he spends flipping truck tires or tearing phone books in half or whatever, and instead do a *musical*, he's going to laugh in my face," I said. "Or worse."

The line went silent for a few seconds before Lou spoke up.

"Well, you're in luck, because I *may* or *may not* have already offered it to him," she said through what I could only assume were clenched teeth.

"What?! Lou!"

"Yep," she said quickly. "In fact, I told him to come to rehearsal tomorrow to observe and have Mr. Hennessy record some of his music. Okay-I-have-to-go-BYEEE!"

I heard her line go dead in my ear. I shook my head and muttered under my breath: "*Lou Benning, you will be the death of me.*"

☆ ☆ ☆ ☆ ☆

I spent the whole next day anxiously awaiting the arrival of Tanner Falzone. When I arrived in the auditorium for our afternoon rehearsal, he was already there, sitting with Lou in the front row. From what I could tell, he seemed to be engaged as he watched us rehearse, following along in his script and even letting out an occasional chuckle. For the last hour of rehearsal, Mr. Hennessy whisked him away to the music room for a private work session.

"So . . . ," I said, approaching him cautiously upon his return to the auditorium. "How'd it go?"

"Pretty good," he said, reaching down to grab his duffel bag. "I took Lou's advice and recorded some voice memos on my phone."

"Oh, that's great, Tanner!" I said enthusiastically. (Despite knowing this guy for a year, I could count on one hand the number of pleasantries we'd actually exchanged.) "So do you think you'll be ready to jump in on Sunday?"

He tugged on his fleece zip-up and looked up at the ceiling. "Should be," he said, giving me a fancy thumbs-up.

"Neat-o," I said with a big cheesy grin, instinctively mimicking his thumbs-up gesture (with a lesser degree of success).

Sunday morning arrived, bringing with it the moment of truth: the moment when Tanner Falzone would open his mouth and determine whether we had a shot at the trophy—or a participation certificate. He stood center stage, a sheet draped haphazardly behind him over a makeshift clothesline, while Mr. Hennessy plunked out the intro to his song.

Tanner closed his eyes and took a deep breath.

"Try to remember the kind of September," a tiny voice wheezed.

I sat in the audience, sandwiched between Lou and Belinda, all three of us straining to listen as our new leading man sang as self-consciously as Louisa stood behind home plate.

"When life was slow and oh, so mellow," Tanner continued, his voice shaky and breathy.

"Um, Lou?" I whispered. "Is this how he usually sounds?"

"I don't know," Lou whispered back. "I assumed he'd have a little more . . . *oomph* to his voice."

"Try to remember the kind of September," Tanner warbled, his voice now becoming strained and slightly sour as he struggled to reach the high notes.

"So you thought he'd be a good El Gallo, even though neither of us have ever even *heard* him sing?" I whispered.

"Well, Big Jule was a non-singing role," she said, "but he still had to sing in the group numbers and he always looked so cocky."

I slumped in my seat, the weight of our hasty decision sinking in. Tanner had already agreed to do the show. We couldn't just take back the offer.

"Breathe, Jack." I felt a bangled hand rest on my shoulder. "It's his first day," Belinda spoke calmly into my ear. "I'm sure he's just nervous."

Tanner Falzone, nervous? The biggest, brashest soccer star of the eighth grade, nervous? I couldn't help but laugh at the thought.

"He's just 'in his head' right now," Belinda whispered. "He's feeling vulnerable. He needs someone to talk him off the ledge."

"How am I supposed to do that?" I pouted. "You want to talk about 'nervous'? That's exactly what *I* feel every time I see him walking toward me in the hallway."

I watched Belinda look over to Lou and then up to the stage where Tanner was choking his way through the final chorus. I shrunk even deeper into the chair, my hands clasped on the side of my head in defeat.

"*Jack*," I felt Belinda's voice whisper in my ear.

I looked up to see her peering at me with kind eyes. "I know you're the director," she said in a low voice, "and I don't want to overstep, but if you'd like," she proceeded cautiously, "maybe . . . *I* could help."

Lou's eyes flashed over to me. It was an understatement to say that Belinda and I used to have a complicated relationship. Luckily, it wasn't the case anymore, and as I watched Tanner sweat under the auditorium lights, I knew I could use an extra hand.

"If you think you can help"—I turned to Belinda—"then go for it. I trust you."

She smiled reassuringly and nodded.

"Try to remember, and if you remember, then follow," Tanner's voice creaked, arriving mercifully at the end of the song. He smiled uncertainly out into the audience.

"That was great, Tanner," Belinda called from the audience. "Jack here has to fill out some forms for the competition. You just wouldn't *believe* the hoops they make you jump through!" she said, eyeing me in her periphery and slipping me her silver pom-pom pen. "So he's asked me to work with you for a little bit."

"Yeah, that was great, Tanner," I said, picking up

her cue and grabbing the pen. "I gotta take care of these ASAP, so if you don't mind working with your old director, I'll be with you in just a minute."

I began fake-scribbling notes in the margins of my script. (It was easier said than done. Her outrageously embellished writing utensil was so top-heavy, it nearly fell out of my hand. How was she able to write with this thing?)

"Uh, okay." Tanner shrugged, wrinkling his forehead.

"So," Belinda said, sitting up in her chair. "I've got a question for you: Why are you singing this song?"

Tanner stared back at her blankly. "Uhh," he grumbled. "To tell people that it's . . . September?"

A couple of giggles emerged from the cast. I looked up skeptically from my fake form-filling-out at Belinda, but she looked anything but ready to throw in the towel.

"That's right." She nodded. "You're the narrator. You're setting the scene. You're bringing us into the world of *The Fantasticks*."

"Oh." Tanner nodded. "Right."

My pen stopped its writing. I began to lean in.

"What if we did a little exercise?" Belinda said.

"Kind of like . . . Oh, what does Coach call them in soccer?" she asked, squinting her eyes. "Oh, right! A *drill*!"

"Um, okay," he said, scratching the back of his neck.

"Yeah, let's sing the song again," Belinda called from the audience. "But this time, let's forget about the music. Instead, I just want you to speak the lyrics."

"Just, like, *talk* them?"

"Precisely." She nodded, her thick red curls bobbing in agreement. "I want you to use them to describe the setting. Help us envision the countryside. What does it look like? Are the leaves on the trees green or just beginning to turn orange? What does it smell like? Don't worry about placement or breathing or any of that extra stuff." She swatted the air with her manicured hands. "I'm still going to have Frank play the music under you, but all I want you to do is just talk to us."

"Just *talk* to you," he repeated. "Okay." He shrugged reluctantly. "If you say so."

"Go ahead, Frank." Belinda nodded to Mr. Hennessy, who in turn began plinking the dreamy intro to the opening number.

"Try to remember," Tanner spoke in a monotone voice, "the kind of September when life was slow . . ."

He sounded completely unenthused, like a robot reading words on a computer screen.

". . . And oh, so mellow."

"What do you *see?*" Belinda shouted from the audience, clasping her fists together.

"Try to remember," he said, rolling his neck and straightening his back, "the kind of September when grass was green."

As Tanner continued to speak, more and more you could detect slight changes. His body seemed to loosen up. His focus began to settle. His lyrics were becoming clearer. As Mr. Hennessy started to play the second verse, Belinda shouted out another prompt to Tanner:

"Imagine you're talking to just one person."

This time as he began to speak, a twinkle appeared in his eye. His words painted images of willows and yellow grain and dreams that are "*kept beside your pillow.*" I couldn't know for sure who he'd chosen to picture, but whoever it was, he was certainly connecting with them. I watched out of the corner of my eye as Lou leaned forward in her seat, resting her chin in her hand.

And as the final verse commenced, the one about hollow hearts and winter snow, I noticed something else, too—even though Tanner wasn't trying to, his speaking voice (which was naturally so big and resonant) began slowly matching the tune being played beneath him.

"Wouldja look at that," I murmured in a low voice.

"Deep in December, our hearts should remember and follow."

Mr. Hennessy's piano faded with the final plink of a cutoff, leaving Tanner staring out into the auditorium, eyes wide, watching perhaps as invisible snow fell from the rafters, covering the audience in a cold white dust. It was magnificent.

I leaned over and whispered two words into Belinda's ear.

"Thank you."

She threw me a wink. "Ah, it was nothing, darlin'."

From that moment on, things began zipping along brilliantly. Rehearsals exploded with new life. Tanner had shaken off his early nerves, and I was directing with a newfound confidence. Our cast began owning their characters, and Belinda was at my side every step of the way, lending an ear whenever I needed to bounce around a new idea. The best part of it all was that everyone seemed genuinely happy to be there.

My proudest moment came at the end of the school week, as we rehearsed one of the sweetest numbers from the show, "Soon It's Gonna Rain." I'd decided to stage it modestly, with Sebastian and Lou crouched on the floor and Jenny above them holding a tree branch. It was clearly Lou and Sebastian's favorite song to sing, and their voices blended perfectly in it. In the final verse, as the characters Matt and Luisa surrendered to the idea of being caught in the storm, I had Jenny reach into her pouch and sprinkle them with tiny blue pieces of paper "rain." It was a simple bit of stagecraft, but paired with the haunting piano accompaniment and beautiful voices, it made me remember the quiet simplicity that drew me to the show in the first place.

☆ ☆ ☆ ☆ ☆

I returned home that evening triumphant, marching up the stairs like I was at Radio City, about to accept a Tony Award.

WANNA FACETIME? I texted Teddy (another activity I'd grown accustomed to).

OF COURSE! he responded.

"How's the show going?" I said into the camera, launching immediately into the world of Ghostlight. "What's it like being the lead this time around?"

"Aw, it's so cool!" He beamed. "Wren has really come up with some great stuff. I knew she was smart, but this is next level."

"That's awesome! What sort of stuff is she doing?" I asked, feeling my curiosity creep in. I wondered if other directors had felt the same kind of breakthrough.

"Well, Cavendish is sort of known at Ghostlight for reinterpreting the classics, so Wren has had to think completely outside the box. Remember how I told you that her dad's a director?"

"Yeah, at Steppenwolf?"

"Exactly," he continued. "Well, what I didn't know was that her mom is, like, an inventor. For phone apps, or something. You know that game *Bubble-opolis*?"

"Yeah, I love that game."

"Her mom invented that!" he cheered. "So she's taken both her dad's influence and her mom's world and kind of made *How to Succeed* about that. She has it set in modern-day Wicker Park, which is this totally hipster neighborhood in Chicago, and instead of it taking place in a 1960s office building, she's made it like we're all working at a new tech start-up. So instead of secretaries, people are app developers, and instead of coffee, everyone's drinking Red Bull."

"Wow," I said, feeling a little flustered. "That's a really cool idea."

"Oh, and you know how my character starts out stuck in the mail room, right?"

"Yeah, totally," I replied. "That 'Company Way' song."

"Right, right," he cut in. "Well, in this version, I'm stuck running the company's Twitter account."

"That's hilarious!" I said, meaning it, but simultaneously feeling a twinge of jealousy sneak into my voice.

"Yeah, we've only had, like, twenty rehearsals, but already I can tell it's going to be amazing. Like, *How to Succeed* is a great show, but she's making it really *mean* something to today's audience."

I could tell he was recycling sound bites, no doubt that had been drilled into the cast by this blue-haired Wren character.

"And she's thinking really big picture, too," he continued. "She's doing this big *commentary* on social media and digital marketing and, oh, what was it?" he said, squinting his eyes. "Oh right, something called *tech dependency*."

I sank into my pillow. I thought back to our rehearsals and the confidence I'd had just one hour ago. The excitement I'd felt when someone sang on pitch or didn't fall on their face doing one of Jenny's dances, it all began to feel stupid in comparison. I hadn't come up with any kind of concept or even realized there was more than one way to do *The Fantasticks*. The more I thought about it, the more I realized that all I was really doing as a director was reading stage directions and translating them into blocking. Suddenly our show I'd imagined sweeping the competition was looking a lot more like something else—a big fat failure.

"How's your show going?" Teddy asked, smiling broadly on the screen.

"Oh," I sat up, trying to dash the look of concern from my face. "It's going really well, too. You know, just working on the material, figuring out the moments."

I'd planned on telling him about the mothers'

slapstick duet and my concept for "Soon It's Gonna Rain," but after hearing about Cavendish's edgy, techno musical, was he really going to be impressed with paper confetti?

"That's so great!" Teddy nodded. "I bet you're, like, the most fun director in the world."

I forced out a smile. "Thanks."

"Ugh," Teddy groaned. "Well, I should go. My parents are dragging me to a gallery opening, and I need to put on a suit."

"You in a suit? That, I gotta see," I said, trying to cover the weird feeling I was suddenly having. "Send pics or it didn't happen."

"Will do!" He laughed. "Wait till you see this hideous tux. I look like a scrawny penguin. See ya, Jack!"

I frowned as Teddy's face disappeared from the screen. Normally when I got off the phone with him I felt giddy, like I was a better, more comfortable version of myself. But right now I felt the opposite. I felt like a little kid. I'd been stupid to think that we could topple Cavendish's winning streak the very first time at bat, especially when my good ideas consisted of getting people to sing their lines loud enough so we could hear them, not even thinking about a "big picture."

I started fearing the worst. What if we showed up at Ghostlight with a piece that looked like it was just thrown together by a bunch of kids? What if I'd dragged Lou into a crummy project when she'd lined up a potentially great one with the Shaker Heights Players? What if Teddy, who seemed so excited to see what I would do as a director, came to realize that I really wasn't special after all?

I wasn't sure what I was supposed to do; I just knew that I needed to talk to someone. I picked up my phone and dialed Lou's number.

"Hey," I said. "Could you come over? I think we're doing everything wrong."

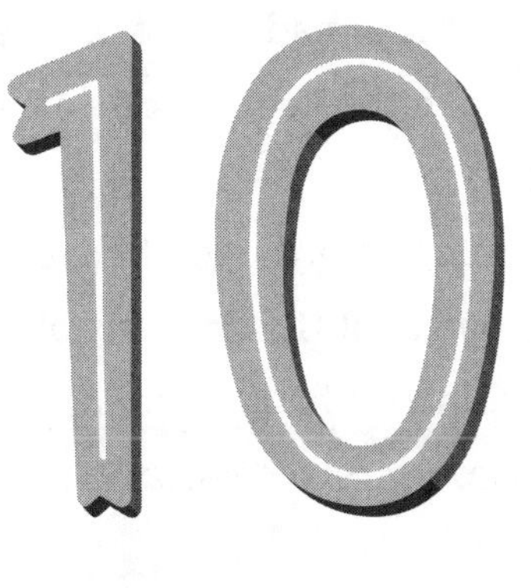

Louisa

I HURRIED OVER TO JACK'S house, thoroughly perplexed. *Doing everything wrong?* How was that possible? Today we'd had one of our best rehearsals yet; Jack had staged "Soon It's Gonna Rain" so beautifully that when Jenny started to sprinkle the "rain" above our heads, I caught Belinda wiping tears from her eyes with the sleeve of her *Cats* sweatshirt. And trust me—Belinda Grier wasn't much for crying. I racked my brain as I approached the Goodriches' front stoop, trying to guess what could have happened over the last two hours that would cause Jack to feel like we were "doing everything wrong" and coming up with nothing. I only had to knock once before Jack swung open the door, anxiously awaiting my arrival.

"Come on in," he ordered, then led me upstairs to his room and shut the door, visibly agitated.

"I don't think we have a chance at winning," he said with deep concern. "Not with the show we've got right now."

"What do you mean?" I asked defensively. "Everyone's doing such a great job."

"Everyone *is* doing a great job," Jack assured me. "You guys are awesome. But you guys are not the problem—*I* am."

"What are you talking about?"

"I was just FaceTiming with Teddy," he said, pacing restlessly around his room. Normally a reference to Teddy would send me into fits of speculation about Jack's love life, but I could tell by his behavior that whatever was bothering him in this moment had little to do with romance.

"They're *way* ahead of us in terms of creativity," he continued, shaking his head. "Their director—"

"Who—*Bird*?"

"*Wren*," he corrected. "She has all these cool ideas about how to make the show 'current.'"

"Current?"

Talking a mile a minute, Jack went on to describe all the things Wren was doing to make her presentation of *How to Succeed*... stand out, like setting the show at a tech start-up company in some park with wicker where everyone drinks Red Bull all day.

"I mean, I'm not doing anything like that!" Jack cried, grabbing his *Fantasticks* script off his desk. "I'm just following the stage directions!" He thumbed through the pages in disgust.

"Hey—you are not 'just following the stage directions,'" I said, thinking of all the ways Jack had impressed me over the last couple of weeks, like how he'd gotten Raj and Radhika to embrace their inner clowns, and how he'd been so collaborative with Jenny, and how patient he'd been with Tanner as he helped him become a leading man. Mostly, though, I was impressed by what a great leader he'd become, always willing to listen to us but also always knowing what he wanted to do. Unfortunately, that confidence had vanished.

"Well," Jack scoffed, "I'm definitely not being as creative as Cavendish."

"Do you think the other schools are trying to be as creative as Cavendish?" I asked. "I mean, it doesn't say anywhere in the Ghostlight guidelines that you have to do something weird with your show, or—what did you say Teddy's school was making? A '*commentary*'?"

I'd always thought that kind of thing only happened in experimental theater, where Shakespeare plays were set in grocery stores, or audience members had to wear masks. I didn't know that it also happened in middle-school musical theater competitions.

"No, I don't think the other schools are doing anything like that, either, which is the problem," Jack said emphatically. "If Cavendish is the only school that's daring to be different, then of course they're going to win again. All the other shows will seem totally boring."

I knew Jack was talking about his own direction, but I still couldn't help feeling a little stung by the suggestion that our presentation was one big snooze-fest.

"What about turning the characters of the fathers into mothers? That's different," I offered, only to have Jack shake his head in dismissal.

"Not different enough. You should have heard Teddy. Everyone's going to be wearing Bluetooth headsets."

I was starting to feel as agitated as Jack, which must have showed, because he stopped pacing for a moment and looked at me in earnest.

"The thing is, Lou, if we were doing a school play, we'd be in great shape. But we're not—we're preparing for a competition. And you said yourself that you weren't going to give up *Sound of Music* unless we beat Cavendish."

That was true. I'd recently learned that Bridget Livak had won the role of Brigitta in *Sound of Music* (why were we all playing characters with our own names?), and while I was genuinely glad that I'd chosen to do *The Fantasticks* instead, I was still a little uncertain about my decision when I thought about the fun Bridget must be having with the Shaker Heights Players. As much as I hated to admit it, my main consolation prize was imagining a glorious victory over Cavendish. Picturing Jack and myself lifting a trophy above our heads, my agitation gave way to a sudden determination.

"Okay, then fine," I said. "Let's come up with our own concept."

"You mean start over?" Jack asked, clearly overwhelmed. "But if we're going to change our presentation, we have to do it, like, right now."

"Yes, we do," I agreed, grabbing Jack's laptop off the floor and handing it to him. "We still have three weeks left of rehearsal, so let's start making a list of ideas." We'd come too far; sacrifices had been made, actors replaced, precious hours devoted to making something of our own. To walk away from it all because of a few intimidating Bluetooth headsets seemed not only nonsensical, but cowardly. We could still win Ghostlight; we just had to be more strategic.

Jack hesitated for a split second, then dutifully turned off his phone, turned on his laptop, and opened one of his notebooks to a blank page. Before turning off my own phone, I texted my mom: ***U & DAD CAN EAT WITHOUT ME.*** I had a feeling Jack and I wouldn't be leaving his room for a while.

"Okay," said Jack warily, his fingers poised above the keyboard, "start brainstorming."

One three-page list, eighty-five Google searches, a quick review of the twentieth and twenty-first centuries as told by our social studies textbooks, plus an entire bag of trail mix later, we found ourselves overwhelmed by half-baked, uninspiring ideas.

The Fantasticks at a carnival?

"They'll wonder why we didn't just do the musical *Carnival*."

The Fantasticks in an insane asylum?

"They did that with a *Sweeney Todd* revival."

The Fantasticks inside a bottle of "Fantastik" household cleaner?

"Huh?"

We were stuck and I hated feeling stuck. There had to be *something* we could do to make *The Fantasticks* unique.

"Ugh," I groaned, "why is this so hard? Maybe we should let an idea appear to us in our dreams." I pressed the heels of my palms into my eyes. The phrase *tortured artist* suddenly felt very fitting.

"Let's zone out for a couple minutes," Jack suggested. "'Cause right now we're thinking too hard."

"Fine."

A bleary-eyed Jack handed me the remote control, then fell back on the floor, draping an arm over his face. I clicked on the television. A rerun of one of those ridiculous reality dating shows was in full swing as a contestant addressed the camera, listing off the qualities he looked for in a girlfriend. As the contestant began to describe himself, boasting about his "romantic side" and his "love of the mountains," Jack sat up with a jolt, stared hard at the screen, then turned slowly to me.

"Lou, you're a genius."

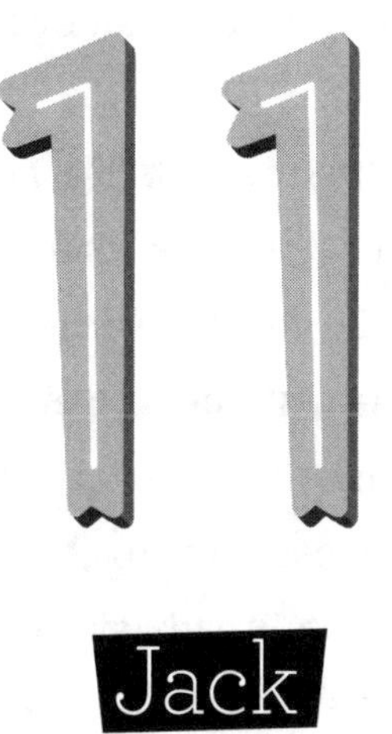

Jack

"IT'S PERFECTLY NORMAL TO be nervous, Jack. But don't you think this is a little drastic?" Belinda said Sunday morning, resting a purple-painted fingernail on the tip of her chin. "I thought what you were doing was great. The cast seemed happy, and there was a real . . . *clarity* in your storytelling."

I nodded politely, stealing a quick glance at the clock in the back of the auditorium. I still had three minutes left to convince her before our cast would begin shuffling in for the Sunday rehearsal.

"Right," I replied. "But we're never going to beat a hundred other schools with the same boring rendition of *The Fantasticks* that everyone is used to seeing."

"Mm-hmm." She frowned. "No, I see your point. And honestly, I like it. I think it's ambitious and it certainly seems like you have a clear vision of what you want." Belinda shifted her weight. "I just worry that three weeks isn't a whole lot of time. I mean, we both know how hard it is to change things when you're in previews on Broadway, but this is a cast of middle-schoolers," she said, throwing me a playful wink. "They aren't nearly as quick on their feet as you and me."

I looked down at my shoes. I wondered if maybe I should have waited for Lou to arrive before pitching Belinda our great new idea.

"Look," she said, dropping her voice. "I know we've had our differences, Jack. And I want to make it clear that at the end of the day this is still *your* show. But as the adult supervisor, I feel it's my job to make sure you're not rushing into a decision."

I let her words sink in. I thought back to my conversation with Teddy, the awful feeling I had in my stomach once I realized how old-school our old-hat production of *The Fantasticks* would look next to Cavendish's ultra-modern take on *How to Succeed*.

The moment Lou and I began hatching our new plan, though, that feeling went away, replaced with excitement about telling our story in a way that felt hot on the cultural pulse.

"Right," I replied, gathering my strength. "And thank you for being so honest. But I think what's most important is that we're able to stand out," I said confidently, rolling my shoulders back. "And I think this is the way to do it."

Belinda peered into my eyes.

"Well, okay then, Jack." She smiled genuinely. "In that case, just know that I'm here to support you, so let me know what I can do to help."

"Thanks, Belinda," I replied, just as the first wave of cast members pushed through the steel doors in the back of the auditorium. "I will."

☆ ☆ ☆ ☆ ☆

"There's a real parallel between the manufactured realities of *The Fantasticks* and reality television," I explained, using the new phrase Lou and I had come up with.

The entire cast was gathered onstage, listening as I pitched the new vision for our competition piece: *The Fantasticks* as a reality TV dating show.

The concept was simple: Matt and Luisa were innocent contestants, unaware that their mothers (two glamorous society women) were scheming to get them together by pretending to hate each other. The character of El Gallo became the smiling, manipulative host, and the Mute became his camera guy, silently filming all of the action. Henry's and Mortimer's characters were no longer aging actors but production assistants working on El Gallo's film crew.

"The words and music will pretty much stay the same, though we may make some cuts to help support the concept," I said, finishing the speech. "Are there any questions? I know this is a lot to take in."

I looked around the room, watching as my words sank in. Eyes squinted and arms crossed, but no one's lips moved, leaving an excruciating silence. I glanced over to Lou, whose tight smile indicated that she was just as anxious about the cast's reaction as I was. Belinda stood off to the side, watching the group with interest and nibbling on the end of her purple gel pen. As I waited for someone to speak up, my mind traveled back to our brainstorming session. Would our midnight idea still hold up in the light of the day?

Finally, a hand slowly inched into the air. Tanner opened his mouth to speak.

"So . . ." He knitted his brow. "We're gonna be on TV?"

A ripple of laughter broke the stillness, and tension left the room like air out of a balloon. Sebastian snorted loudly and shook his head. "No, stupid, we're gonna *pretend* to be on TV."

"Oh," said Tanner, his hand sinking quietly before he shot it up a second time. "So how does that change what we do?"

"Well," I began, "the first thing we need to do is get Jenny a camera."

☆☆☆☆☆

Once the cast had moved on to technical questions—Sarah and Esther wanted to know if the scheming society moms were from New Jersey or Orange County—Lou joined me in the front row for a one on one.

"That went really well!" she exclaimed. "You hit on everything we talked about, and I think the cast is really into it."

"I dunno," I said, shuffling my script and blocking notes. "I feel like there were a lot of confused faces."

"They just haven't heard all of your great ideas," she assured me. "I promise, once we get everything on its feet, it will all make sense."

☆ ☆ ☆ ☆ ☆

"Let's start at the very beginning," I announced to the room.

"A very good place to start," a smattering of voices whispered to themselves.

"Just like in the old version," I continued. "We're going to begin with Tanner singing 'Try to Remember,' but this time, we're going to add Jenny to the scene."

I looked over to the wings where Jenny stood, a shoe box tucked under her arm as a stand-in for the camera.

"Now, Tanner, instead of speaking to the audience, I want you to look directly into Jenny's camera. Think of it like the beginning of a TV show where the host introduces the challenge and contestants."

Tanner scooted to his spike mark downstage center.

"Do you watch any dating shows?" I asked him. "*Wife Island*? *Boy Meets Girls*? *Wingman, Inc.*?"

Tanner crossed his arms and gave me a withering look.

"What do *you* think?"

"Right . . . ," I said, nodding my head. "Well, how about . . . a game show? You must watch a couple of those."

Tanner shrugged his shoulders. "I guess I like that *Trash Titans* show."

"The one where they build robots out of stuff they find in a landfill and then make them fight each other?"

"Yeah," he said, his eyes glazing over as he stared into the middle distance, presumably picturing old microwaves dueling to the death. *"So cool."*

"Perfect!" I said, taking the baton. "So, how does the host of that show talk? Does he have a catchphrase or something?"

Tanner began to grin, clearing his throat and throwing his head back in a big cartoony motion. "Weeeee-eeelcome back to another episode of *Trash Titans*," he said in a corny announcer voice. "I'm your host, Harley Sampson, and it's time to Build. Those. BOTS!"

"That's the voice!" I cheered.

"Yeah." Tanner laughed. "My mom says I sound just like him."

"No, I mean, *that's* the voice," I said. "The voice I want you to use for El Gallo!"

"You serious?" He cocked his head.

"Dead serious. Let's jump right in."

I waved Jenny over and motioned for her to crouch on the floor (which she did, somewhat reluctantly).

"Now, I want you to point that camera right at Tanner's face," I said, stepping back to admire the new stage picture I'd composed. "All right, let's try this."

Mr. Hennessy began playing the intro of the song, and Tanner fixed his gaze into the top corner of the shoe box.

"Trrrrrrry to remember the kind of September—"

As we dove deeper into the script, it was hard not to notice that the cast's initial skepticism was beginning to thaw. Tanner started playing around with more Harley Sampson affectations, while Jenny began circling around him, changing her angles like a professional camerawoman.

Admittedly, sometimes we got to a scene where the concept wasn't totally clear—

"Why am I talking about watering vegetables when we're supposed to be on a soundstage?" Sarah asked as we began the scene with the mothers.

"Let's just cut that whole gardening subplot," I suggested. "Maybe just . . . mime putting on makeup or something."

"Do I still fight off El Gallo even though he's supposed to be the TV host?" Sebastian asked as we moved on to the kidnapping scene.

"You know, I'm gonna have to get back to you on that one," I said, flipping through my script. "Let's skip over that for now, and we'll circle back later."

So I hadn't answered *every* question, but it was still the first day.

"All right, gang," I said, moving on to the next scene on my worklist. "Let's take our places for the beginning of 'Much More.' And this time, Lou," I said, reaching into my pocket and pulling out my phone, "let's try taking some selfies during the chorus."

Louisa

OH, IT HAD SOUNDED LIKE such a great idea in Jack's bedroom! And for the first week of rehearsals after Jack's introduction of the reality-show concept, it really did seem like we had come up with something smart—something that could set us apart from the rest of our Ghostlight competitors. A lot of Jack's ideas worked perfectly, like making Jenny the camerawoman, and turning songs like "Much More" into video testimonials. But by the beginning of the second week, the questions that Jack couldn't answer still hung in the air, and what was worse—new questions kept popping up.

"If we're not supposed to be actors anymore, then why am I still quoting Shakespeare plays?"

It was Sunday afternoon—we'd be leaving for Ghostlight on Friday—and Raj didn't realize I could hear him. He and Radhika and I were all standing in the wings, but a long piece of black velour masking (separating me from them) must have made Raj feel like he was having a private conversation. I looked out onto the stage where Jack and Tanner were reviewing "Try to Remember" and held my breath as I listened to Radhika's response to her brother.

"It makes no sense," she said, sounding worried. "And why would Mortimer keep pretending to die if she is just a PA on a television set? What is the purpose?"

(It seemed like every piece of Jack's direction was now met with the question *Why?*, requiring him to spend precious minutes explaining his decisions instead of actually directing.)

"I don't know," Raj said quietly, "but I am starting to think we will look foolish."

Upon hearing the word *foolish*, I winced. As the person who had helped Jack come up with the new idea for the show, I felt a certain responsibility to help my castmates understand that what we were doing would give us an advantage over our competition. The problem was that it was getting harder and harder to defend Jack's choices, since I, too, was starting to think we might end up looking "foolish." I could totally make sense of singing "Much More" to a camera. But I had a harder time making sense of Jack's decision to keep the characters of Luisa and Matt from seeing each other until they sang "Soon It's Gonna Rain" together toward the end of Act One. Jack kept saying that in order for it to seem like a convincing reality dating show, Luisa and Matt ("the two contestants") shouldn't interact at the beginning. But that meant cutting the scene in which the audience gets to see how much they love each other. To me it felt like a dangerous cut to make.

Still, what could I do? Tell my best friend that the show seemed to be getting worse instead of better? After I had strongly encouraged him to change course? Rather than say anything, I'd just started avoiding Jack as much as I could during rehearsals, for fear of betraying what I really thought.

"It's kind of funny, you know?" I suddenly heard Tanner say to Jack, prompting Mr. Hennessy to stop playing. I tried my best to block out Raj and Radhika's quiet worries on the other side of the masking so I could give my full attention to what was happening onstage.

"What is?" Jack asked, digging his hands into his pockets. I could tell he was already wary of whatever Tanner was about to say.

"It's just," Tanner continued, "I'm supposed to be this artificial-type host guy now, and none of what's happening in the story really matters to me, and that's just funny, 'cause it's like the complete *opposite* of what Belinda had me do when I first started."

Jack glanced furtively at Belinda, who sat quietly in the fourth row of the auditorium. I knew she'd had serious doubts about Jack's plans when he first pitched her the reality-show idea, though her concerns mostly had to do with time management. I wondered now if those concerns had grown. Given her complicated history with Jack, though, it was hard to predict whether she would say much to discourage him.

"Uh, what do you mean?" Jack asked, returning his attention to Tanner.

"Like all the connecting stuff, y'know? Like

when she said to picture singing to someone I know . . . ?"

I couldn't be sure, but it seemed like Tanner might have glanced in my direction when he said "someone I know." Maybe I was just hopeful. Either way, I felt a twinge of sadness as I thought back to Tanner's first time singing the opening number, and how, under Belinda's patient direction, he had experienced a real breakthrough, allowing himself to be vulnerable onstage. Now that Jack wanted Tanner's performance to be more superficial, and only about his relationship to the camera/audience, there was no opportunity for him to show any vulnerability at all.

"Well," Jack said, doing his best to not sound defensive, "I still want everything that you're singing to make sense to you. So, it's not the 'complete opposite' of what Belinda had you do before. But keeping you emotionally detached from the story definitely helps—"

"—with the concept, yeah, okay," Tanner interrupted with a wry smile.

"Exactly," said Jack, his eyes darting between Tanner, Belinda, and Mr. Hennessy. "So are we cool to move on?"

☆☆☆☆☆

By Wednesday Jack had settled on a way to answer the remaining unanswerable questions: Whatever didn't work, got cut. Not surprisingly this didn't go over so well.

"You want to scrap the *entire* abduction sequence?"

An hour into rehearsal, after more than half of Raj and Radhika's first scene had been cut, Jenny's choreography was next on the chopping block.

"I want to *adjust* it," Jack replied hastily, knowing how hard Jenny had worked on the number. "It's tricky to have the story set inside a television show and have everyone do these classical ballet moves—it just doesn't make sense." Jenny's clenched jaw must have scared Jack a little, because he added weakly, "You can still have Luisa do a couple ballet moves. But everyone else really should do more contemporary stuff."

Before Jenny could even respond, Jack walked over to Sarah and Esther to re-block their newly trimmed scenes, leaving me alone to deal with Jenny's frustration.

"First of all, they aren't classical ballet moves;

they're traditional musical-theater combinations *rooted* in ballet," she grumbled, citing her thorough research of musical theater choreography. "Second: '*contemporary stuff*'? Jack knows I don't do 'contemporary stuff.' What does he expect me to come up with when we have, like, no time left? A Beyoncé video?"

"Don't stress about it too much, Jenny," I said, trying to sound encouraging. "You just have to change some of your choreography—"

"Lou, please—we're not *changing* anything, we're just *getting rid of* it."

"But what we're doing instead really will work better with the concept."

"Ugh, this *concept*," Jenny drawled sarcastically. "I'm sorry, Lou, but I am getting *so* sick of that word."

You and everyone else, I thought woefully as I watched her walk to the edge of the stage and hop off, searching the rows of seats for her water bottle. No doubt she wanted to rinse out the bad taste left behind from uttering the word *concept*. I looked past Jenny to see Belinda, still quietly watching all of us. Was she ever going to say anything?

More and more cuts were made, stoking

the fires of Raj and Radhika's doubts, Tanner's observations, Jenny's frustration, and Belinda's silence. But all of it paled in comparison to Jack's final, and most devastating, decision. On Friday, the day before we were set to leave for Ghostlight, he gathered us on the stage after we'd finished our final run-through.

"All right, guys," he began, his voice low and gravelly with exhaustion. "I know it's been an intense couple of weeks, but I really appreciate all of your patience. Thanks for working so hard; I think it's going to pay off this weekend."

I looked around at my castmates' faces. No one seemed terribly convinced. I wondered if Jack could tell.

"One last thing, and then I'll let everyone go home and pack," he said, then cleared his throat and looked over our heads, toward the Exit sign, "we're going to cut 'Soon It's Gonna Rain.'"

An excruciating silence followed, during which I felt the eyes of my castmates fixed on me and Sebastian, awaiting a response. Finally, from the edge of the stage came the voice I'd been waiting to hear.

"You sure you want to do that, Jack?"

Belinda, leaning against the proscenium arch with her legs crossed in front of her, looked genuinely worried. It was the same expression she'd had in my living room last spring when she thought our production of *Guys and Dolls* might be over.

"It's just," she added gently, "you did such beautiful work with that number. That's all."

Jack took a deep breath and dug his hands deep into his pockets. Would he be able to hear her comments without getting defensive? Would he be able to see that he was making a huge mistake?

"Thanks," Jack said. "It's just . . . watching it now, I realize . . . if we really do want to keep Matt and Luisa separated until the end, if we're trying to make the statement that technology keeps us all disconnected . . . even in the pursuit of love . . . then leaving that song in the show just won't work for the . . ." Not even Jack could bring himself to say *concept*—it had become too toxic a word. Belinda nodded slowly.

"Well, if you think it's for the best," was all she said.

The tears that had threatened to spill down my cheeks at first were now displaced by a surge of anger. Not only had my favorite part of the show just been eliminated, but our *very experienced* faculty advisor had *very politely* given Jack the perfect opportunity to change his mind, and he hadn't. I inhaled sharply through my nose, not wanting the rest of my cast to see how upset I'd become. After all, none of us had been spared, had we? We'd all had to sacrifice parts of our performances for the sake of Jack's vision.

"Plus," Jack added halfheartedly, "it keeps our running time well within the limits of the competition rules, so that's good."

"Bet it doesn't feel good," Jenny whispered in my ear, squeezing my shoulder as she walked past me toward the lip of the stage, and just like that—the weight of everything that had been changed and taken away from us over the last three weeks was more than I could bear. As I followed Jenny into the audience to get my bag and coat, I knew that I couldn't leave without saying something to Jack. Not wanting to make a scene, however, I would have to wait until everyone, including Belinda, had left. As soon as the heavy double doors clicked shut behind Esther (always slow), I walked back down the aisle toward the stage, where Jack was

thumbing through his script in the front row.

"I can't believe you're cutting that song," I called out, startling him. He stood and turned to face me, looking both nervous and tired.

"You know I'm not doing it to be mean, right?" he said, offering a weak smile.

"No, I know," I said, "it's just—"

"I really think the whole piece will work better without it," Jack interrupted, feeding me the same line he'd used each time he made a cut.

"Yeah, but it was one of the best moments in the presentation. Belinda even said so," I said, trying my best to remain calm.

"Well sure," he conceded, "in the old version."

My attempt at calm vanished as I snapped back, "In any version."

We stared at each other for a moment, silently acknowledging that we had stepped into uncomfortable territory. Finally, Jack broke the tension with a shrug.

"Well, if I thought that were true, then . . ." He hesitated.

"Then what?"

"Then I would have kept it in."

I didn't want to be mad at my friend; I really

didn't. But when Jack said stuff like that, it made me furious. I flashed to the image of my castmates as they exited, all looking worn-out, uncertain, and defeated. The competition wouldn't officially begin until Saturday, but we were already acting like losers.

"You know what *is* true?" I asked, no longer able to contain my anger, "nobody thinks this new version is working."

Jack's face hardened.

"You mean the version you said we *had* to do if we wanted to win?"

Oh I see, I thought, *he's going to try to make all of this my fault.*

"You called me over to your house that night because you were freaking out, remember?" I said, my palms starting to sweat. "I was just trying to help you figure out what to do."

"Right, but only because you wanted to make sure we beat Cavendish."

"And you told me that wasn't possible with the show we had! So what was I supposed to say?"

"I don't know, but don't forget that you're the one who's been obsessed with winning Ghostlight from the beginning. Changing our show was just as much your idea as it was mine."

"It wasn't my idea to cut 'Soon It's Gonna Rain.'"

"Which is the only reason you're mad, isn't it? Because I cut your song?"

Ouch.

"No," I said slowly, "I'm mad because our show doesn't work anymore. We messed it up."

"You mean *I* messed it up."

Maybe that is what I meant. Either way, it didn't matter. It suddenly occurred to me that assigning blame at this late hour wouldn't accomplish anything but hurting people's feelings. I looked down at the floor, feeling slightly ashamed but still angry, too.

"Whatever," I said softly. "It's too late now, anyway."

"Awesome," Jack said, his voice thick with sarcasm. "Thanks for your support, Lou."

I looked up to see that Jack was regarding me with an expression I'd never seen before: a horrible mix of disappointment and disgust. It was the kind of expression that made me think we might never make up.

"It's not just my song. It's Sebastian's, too," was all I said as I turned and walked up the aisle to the exit doors.

☆☆☆☆☆

Outside my mom was waiting for me in the car. As soon as I slid into the passenger seat, she started talking a mile a minute.

"Okay, so all of my stuff is packed for the weekend," she began, her voice buoyant, "which means I'm at your disposal this evening. If you need anything ironed, let me know. Your father has also volunteered to run out for any last-minute items you might need. And he's offered to take us out to dinner if you like, as a good-luck send-off. I think he's a little jealous that he's not coming with us this weekend." She turned to me with a grin.

"So—you guys ready for your big weekend?"

Not even a little bit, I thought miserably, wishing I shared an ounce of my mom's enthusiasm. Normally I told my mom everything, but I was feeling so awful about what had just happened with Jack that I couldn't bring myself to talk about it.

"Yeah, mostly nervous, though," I replied, silently acknowledging that at least half of my response was true. I was definitely nervous.

"Well, *sure*," said Mom. "Even us parents are nervous."

As she proceeded to tell me about the phone conversations she'd had with the other parent chaperones that day, I heard my own phone buzzing from inside my backpack. I pulled it out only to discover that Jack and I had missed about a dozen text messages from Teddy and Kaylee, who were unable to contain their excitement about our imminent reunion. My stomach began to ache as I scrolled through the most recent texts.

TEDDY: *GOODRICH?? BENNING?? WHERE R U GUYS??*

KAYLEE: *LAST TIME I CHECKED THIS THREAD WAS CALLED THE "FOUR MUSKETEERS"?!*

TEDDY: *HAVE YOU CRACKED UNDER THE PRESSURE?*

KAYLEE: *R U GUYS TOO "FANTASTICK" TO TALK TO US ANYMORE?*

TEDDY: *SERIOUSLY, SHOULD WE BE WORRIED?*

KAYLEE: *HELLOOOO?*

TEDDY: *???????*

KAYLEE: *??????????*

Jack

I'VE ALWAYS HATED THE BUS. The sticky floor and grease-smeared glass, the dull gray pleather and the way your body is hurled out of its seat every time you hit a pothole. Maybe it comes from being raised in the city, where the easiest way to get around was an underground train that ran twenty-four hours a day, but I've learned to avoid buses at all costs. On those rare occasions when we did have to take the M60 bus to LaGuardia Airport, it was only a matter of time before the stop-start-stop-start bus route turned me as green as a traffic light.

The bus to Columbus was no exception—but

this time, I couldn't blame my queasiness on speed bumps, a broken air conditioner, or a cranky driver named Larry.

The stench of dread hung in our yellow SHMS school bus like a rotten egg. Ever since our big overhaul of *The Fantasticks*, everyone in the cast seemed to be on edge.

Our parents and chaperones chatted casually up front, while the cast occupied the back of the bus, stewing over my hasty production choices. Raj and Radhika ran through their lines hurriedly, still confused about whether their production assistants were supposed to be speaking in Shakespearean accents. Jenny glowered in a row by herself with earbuds on full volume, exasperated about having her choreography changed yet again. Worst of all, Lou, the person who helped me come up with the concept in the first place, had barricaded herself in the last row and had been giving me the silent treatment since the previous afternoon. So much for spending the two-and-a-half-hour trip singing "99 Bottles of Beer on the Wall"—the entire bus was a chorus of silence.

It might have been for the best. After our fight the night before, I couldn't imagine what Lou and

I would even say to each other. At this point, the only one talking to me was a taunting voice in my head, whispering menacing thoughts with greater and greater frequency: *You've made a mistake. You're in over your head. You ran out of time.*

Of course, it wasn't (only) the presentation that was giving me anxiety. I knew that once we arrived at the Marriott in Columbus, I'd be greeted by a certain someone—a someone I was excited to see, of course, but as each minute passed, the pressure to make our meeting perfect was making me feel like a shaken can of soda, ready to burst.

Maybe it was the dream that had me so shaken up. The night before we'd departed for Columbus, I dreamt the worst nightmare I'd had since I was in the third grade and had a recurring night terror that Sutton Foster had me blacklisted from the industry after I spilled cranberry juice on her dress at the Tonys. In last night's dream, I was alone on a pitch-black stage, the hot glow of a single stage light beaming down on me. Out of nowhere, a group of faceless kids, all in prep-school uniforms, emerged from the darkness. The house lights came up all at once, and the seats of the cavernous theater were filled into the mezzanine with other faceless kids in blazers and neckties, each of them pointing a single, accusatory finger.

Then, in the front row of the theater, a single figure snapped into focus. It was Teddy, but also *not* Teddy—instead of his ever-present crooked smile, his face was plastered with a cruel, unfamiliar grimace. Not-Teddy walked up to the stage, his dark brown loafers sinking into the thick, floral carpet with every step. He started laughing, and it grew louder and louder as the rest of the theater joined him. The last thing I saw before I woke up, panting like I'd run a marathon and my sheets drenched with sweat, was Not-Teddy throwing his head back and howling like a maniac.

"Tough gig, huh?" Belinda's voice startled me back to the real world. "You doin' all right, darlin'? You look a little green," she said, squeezing into my row.

"No, I'm fine," I said, making room for her. "I just don't like buses. They make me a little carsick."

"Ah." She nodded, looking down at her hands, flexing and curling her ringed fingers before turning back to me. "You know, I remember the first time I ever directed anything. It was a production of *Annie* at my friend's dance studio in Paramus, New Jersey. I thought it would be so easy, just stick all those kids in the right places and tell them to sing, but nooo. Everyone's got *questions*. Everyone's got *opinions*. And no matter what, you can't please them all."

She sighed. "It's a lonely business, Jack, and it's sure not always easy. And mind you, these were ten-year-olds."

"Huh." I blinked.

"It seems like your cast is a little bit"—Belinda squinted her eyes—"*on edge* right now."

"Understatement of the century." I slumped into my seat.

"Jack, they're upset because they're scared, is all," Belinda continued. "But I want you to know that I'm not upset with you in the least."

"You're not?" I said, looking up to her.

"Of course not!" She laughed. "I think what you're doing is brave. Now, have I been a little concerned that you maybe bit off more than you can chew?" She raised an eyebrow. "I think the answer is: *probably*, but I admire your spunk."

We sat in silence for a moment, the hum of the bus engine filling the emptiness of conversation.

"So, what did you end up doing?" I said, finally. "With those ten-year-olds?"

"Oh." She shrugged. "I don't know. Same thing directors always do: Go with your gut and hope for the best."

I looked out the window. As a passing town whooshed by in a blur of gray cement and fall foliage, Belinda's words replayed in my head like lyrics to a song. *Go with your gut and hope for the best*. I wasn't sure if they were meant to be encouraging. If my gut was any indication of how our performance would be received, right now we were headed straight for the crapper.

"Now, on another note," she said. "Try taking your thumb and pointer finger and pressing the area on your palm like this," she said, pinching the fleshy bit of skin on her opposite hand. "When I did the bus-and-truck of *Will Rogers Follies*, I used to get carsick all the time and this always helped!"

☆ ☆ ☆ ☆ ☆

The lobby of the Marriott looked like one of those postapocalyptic movies where hundreds of bewildered people gathered in a public place to take shelter. But instead of hiding from an asteroid or hordes of flesh-eating zombies, the crowds were exchanging hotel keys and handing out welcome packets. Everywhere I looked, kids were rolling suitcases or piling into elevators or splashing around near the fountain. While our parents gathered at the check-in desk, sorting out room assignments and meal vouchers, I stood alone, going over the latest texts on my phone for the sixth time.

Lou: *We've arrived! When can we meet up?*

Kaylee: *We're about to roll up. Don't make any new best friends without me!*

Teddy: *Unpacking now. See you in a few!*

An entire *42nd Street*–size ensemble of butterflies was performing a quick change in my stomach. It wouldn't be long before I'd see Teddy. In a matter of minutes, I'd hear his voice again, and marvel at the way he overemphasized his *t*'s, and smell his shirt as he leaned in for a hug, smelling like clean laundry and library books. But these warm thoughts were snuffed out by that voice looming in my head.

But, Jack . . . what if he doesn't feel the same way about you?

"We're on the fourth floor," my mom said, walking over to our group and handing out key cards to the chaperones. "Also, Jack, they said you need to check in at the ballroom to go over technical stuff with the stage manager."

"Oh." I slumped, my thoughts returning to the unsettling world of *The Fantasticks*.

"Would you like Belinda or me to come with you?" my mom asked.

I looked over to Lou. Normally, this would be just the type of errand she'd volunteer to accompany me on, but the cloudy look on her face told me that this time I was on my own.

"No, it's fine," I said, turning back to my mom and the rest of the cast. "You guys can start unpacking. It should only take a minute."

I handed off my suitcase and slowly made my way to the enormous ballroom in the back of the hotel, dodging groups of MTNs shaking hands and pushing racks of costumes and singing three-part harmonies to "The Schulyer Sisters" from *Hamilton*. As I entered the room, I got the strange feeling that I'd been here before. The uniformed kids, the floral carpeting . . . it was just like my nightmare.

I stopped dead in my tracks. Through the sea of clipboards and lanyards, I saw them—students in identical maroon blazers, crisp khakis, and navy blue ties with canary-yellow stripes. Standing in a circle at the center of the ballroom, they were joking around with one another in a self-assured way that made it obvious they knew more than a few eyes were on them.

All at once, the laughter and roughhousing seemed to halt. At the center of the group, surrounded by kids who looked like they'd stepped out of a Brooks Brothers advertisement, I spotted him. His jacket was slung casually over his shoulder, his shirtsleeves rolled up to the elbows, showing off his tanned arms. His eyes seemed brighter than I'd remembered, his hair shinier and his teeth whiter. As I scrambled to run my fingers through my hair and smooth out the wrinkles on my T-shirt, Teddy turned his head, scanning the room like he knew someone was watching.

I scrunched my eyes shut, bracing myself for the nightmare to begin taking shape, but when I opened them, there was no audience of taunting kids. Just one boy jogging toward me, smiling his crooked smile and reaching his arms wide, pulling me into a hug.

"Jack Attack!" Teddy shouted, wrapping his

arms around my shoulders. Before I got a chance to memorize the brush of his hair against my cheek, he'd already pulled away. "How amazing is this place?" he asked breathlessly, gesturing to the crowd of MTNs.

"It's . . . it's . . . ," I muttered, wiping my palms on the front of my jeans. "It's great."

Teddy tilted his head. "You okay, buddy? You look a little green."

"No," I said, straightening the collar of my shirt self-consciously. "No, I'm fine. I'm just a little queasy from the bus ride."

"Aw, feel better, gurgle-guts," Teddy said, giving my sneaker a little kick with his loafers.

I tried my best to let out an agreeable laugh.

"Where's Thing Two?" he asked, looking around the room.

"Who, Lou?" I asked. "Oh, she's up in her room unpacking. But she'll be so jealous I got to see you." I smiled weakly.

"Yeah, Kaylee's supposedly pretty close, too. I can't believe we're all here!"

"Teddy!" a cluster of voices called from the group of uniformed students. He looked to them and then back to me apologetically.

"Sorry," he said, nodding toward the group. "I should probably get back. Cavendish always does this thing where we give each other Paper Plate Awards the night before the competition, but I was thinking we should all meet before the big concert tonight?"

"Yeah, that would be awesome," I said, sounding not quite as excited as I should have.

"That way we can all sit together and catch up before the circus begins tomorrow." He smiled. "How does that sound?"

"Great!" I responded with as much energy as I could muster.

"Perfect," he said, clapping me on the shoulder. "I'll meet you guys outside of the event center!"

And just like that, he was gone, absorbed back into the group of uniformed kids, heading off to some distant corner of the hotel to congratulate one another on how great their show was.

"So I have the script you sent along with your application," the woman holding a clipboard said from behind a folding table piled high with paperwork. She wore a headset, a walkie-talkie, and a name tag that read "TRISH: TECHNICAL DIRECTOR" in big capital letters.

"Is this still the version you're going to use?" she asked, holding up a printed packet.

"Oh." I fished around in my director's folder for a copy of the new and . . . "improved" version of *The Fantasticks*. "No, *this* is actually the updated version," I said, handing her a fresh copy.

"*A boy. A girl. Two fathers. And a wall—a Facebook wall,*" she read off the first page. "Heh, that's funny," she said, kind of half laughing. "Are you guys doing some modern take on a show, too?"

"Yeah," I replied. "Well, sort of. It kind of takes place in a reality show, but there's also social media, too, and then at the end there's, like, this big grand prize."

As I spoke I realized just how weak and confusing my pitch sounded.

"Uh . . . huh," Trish said. "Yeah, I just checked in Cavendish Prep, and they went super modern, too." Her eyes lit up. "I couldn't *believe* their tech requirements. Please tell me you didn't *also* bring fifteen computer monitors, a projector, and a sixty-inch LED screen? Because we only have so many extension cords."

"No," I said hesitantly. "Well, we have some phones and a video camera, but they don't need power sources or anything."

"Phew!" Trish laughed, swiping her hand across her forehead. "Those Cavendish kids sure know how to make my life more complicated. But I gotta say, I'm excited to see what they do this year. *How to Succeed* seems like the perfect musical to set in present day."

What followed was an awkward silence that could have filled the entire overture of *Gypsy*.

"Aaalso, *The Fantasticks*," Trish said, looking down at our script. "Hmm." She frowned. "Yeah, I'll be interested to see how you guys pull this off."

I walked back to my hotel room in a cloud of frustration. It felt like everywhere I looked, kids were having the time of their lives. The hallways were scattered with girls (and the occasional boy) doing the splits, stretching and gossiping with their teammates. Every time I passed a group of students, I caught fragments of conversation—*"she's a soprano," "do you tumble?" "like an eighth-grade Kelli O'Hara."* Laughter filled every elevator and sing-alongs seemed to erupt from every open doorway. Every cheer of glee only seemed to highlight the fact that at the moment, I was feeling exactly the opposite. I'd chosen to do Ghostlight so I could hang out with my friends and create something fun, but all I seemed to be having was regrets about my show and a stupid crush on a boy I was too embarrassed to tell anyone about. The voice in my head began to mock me once again: *You could've been doing* The Sound of Music . . .

☆ ☆ ☆ ☆ ☆

The welcome concert was set to take place in the big event center attached to the hotel. According to our welcome packet, it promised to feature "songs and medleys from Broadway performers" wedged between "instructions and announcements from the Ghostlight staff." Our parents went in to save seats, forcing me and Lou to face each other for the first time, alone. Rather than engage in what promised to be as awkward an interaction as my plot-summary session with Trish, we both buried our noses in our phones, swiping away in silence as we waited for the rest of the Four Musketeers to join us.

Kaylee was the first to arrive after us, greeting Lou and me with a huge hug that made me feel momentarily better.

"I can't believe you're actually here!" she cheered. "Isn't this place slammin'?"

"It's incredible," Lou said, putting on a big plastered smile. "I feel like I'm in Disney World, and not just because Sierra Boggess is about to sing for us."

It took every ounce of my existence *not* to roll my eyes.

"How's your competition piece shaping up?" Kaylee asked.

Lou's face stiffened, so I jumped in. "It's great. We did a modern take on *The Fantasticks* that makes a lot of commentary on the genre of reality TV."

Much better, I thought. Since my earlier gaffe, I'd been practicing the pitch.

"Whoa." She gulped. "You guys are so smart. We're just doing *Once on This Island* with a few folding chairs and some pieces of cloth."

Right at that moment, Teddy's head popped up behind Lou and Kaylee, his arms slung across their shoulders.

"Hey, Musketeers!" he said, grinning like a Cheshire cat.

"Teddy!" both the girls squealed, hugging him around the waist.

"Long time no see," he said, throwing a quick glance my way.

"Everybody hold right there," Kaylee said, whipping out her phone. "There are, like, no good pictures of the four of us from CCU, and I want to remember this moment."

She reached out her arm and snapped a picture of our squad. I wondered if the photo captured my forced smile, or the gap Lou made to keep herself from having to touch me.

"So, Teddy, how doth the Royal Cavendish Academy fare on this eve of competition?" she said, putting on an affected Shakespearean accent and a comical smirk.

"Oh, very well, m'lady," Teddy said, rolling his eyes. "Excited for tomorrow. Did you guys look at the schedule? We're all performing back-to-back."

"I know," Lou said. "I'm glad we're first. I would be so nervous having to perform after watching you guys."

"Are you joking?" Teddy rolled his eyes. "From everything Jack's told me, it's all of *us* that need to watch out for *you*."

Lou caught my eye. It was just for a second before turning back to our friends—*"Aw, come on, YOU'RE the amazing ones"*—but in that moment I could see clearly the profound look of disappointment in her eyes. I felt rotten. These three people were the whole reason I'd fought to do Ghostlight in the first place. Yet here we were, unable to enjoy it for even a second.

"I just want to say," I chimed in, trying to force out a congenial smile, "that no matter what happens tomorrow, I'm really—"

But I was cut off by a girl wedging her way into our circle.

"Oh, *there* you are, Teddy."

The newly arrived stranger had long wavy blond hair and a dash of freckles across her nose. She wore an oversize, unbuttoned Cavendish Prep polo that practically fell off her bare shoulder. Around her neck was a long gold chain with an antique-looking owl pendant at the end.

"Are these your camp friends?" she asked, tucking her hand in the crook of Teddy's elbow.

"Uh, yeah," he said, placing an arm behind her back, sort of presenting her to our group. "This is Juniper. She's playing Rosemary opposite me in *How to Succeed*."

"Aw, nice to meet you," Lou and Kaylee chimed,

taking turns shaking her hand. I reached mine out to shake, but Juniper had already turned back to Teddy, fanning her hands frantically in front of her face. "Oh my *gosh*, Teddy!"

My hand-shaking arm left hanging, I tried to play it off like I had meant to inspect my cuticles instead. It was moderately convincing.

"You'll never *believe* what Aspen just pointed out," she squealed. "My name is *literally* Juniper and I'm playing someone named *Rosemary*!" She giggled. "Isn't that *bananas*?"

"Oh," Teddy replied. "Right, because they're both—"

"—herbs," Juniper cut in. "Yeah, I'm such a nerd for never noticing."

I watched as Teddy's hand traveled down to the small of her back.

"Juniper's dad works with my mom," he said to the three of us. "We've been in the same class since, like, kindergarten."

"But," said Juniper, lifting a finger and poking his cheek, "we've never gotten to play opposite each other in a show until this year. Isn't that *bananas*?"

Kaylee and Lou exchanged a quick look.

"Totally *bananas*," Kaylee replied.

"Well, it was *so* nice meeting you guys," Juniper said, doing a kind of *demi-plié*. "Teddy, don't take *too* long. I saved you a seat!"

All of our heads turned toward Teddy, who suddenly seemed incredibly interested in the pattern of the hotel carpet. *Saved him a seat?* Wasn't Teddy sitting with us? Wasn't that the whole point of meeting out here before? I could feel my face turning red-hot.

"Um." Teddy gulped, raising his head toward her and sort of raising his eyebrows and shrugging. "I kinda told my camp friends I'd sit with them?" He made it sound like a question.

"Aww," Juniper moaned, her mouth turning into an exaggerated pout. "Well, I *guess* that's okay. But maybe at intermission you can come and sit with your *actual* cast."

She twirled around and swanned away toward the concert hall before Teddy had a chance to reply, leaving a bouquet of lavender-scented shampoo in her wake.

"Ohhh maah Gaaa," Kaylee howled once the four of us were alone again. "Teddy, that girl is the *most*!"

"Juniper?" Teddy asked, his face flushing. "Yeah, she's, kind of . . . attached to me."

"Honey, if she were any more attached to you, the two of you could star in a revival of *Side Show*." Kaylee chuckled. "She's, like, *in love*."

I bit the inside of my cheek so hard that I winced.

"Oh, I dunno." Teddy looked down at his feet. "She just gets . . . excited. She's actually really sweet."

Teddy looked extremely uncomfortable, and the group went silent. He dug his hands into the pockets of his khakis and pursed his lips. I recognized that look—the way your body seized up when someone talked about a person you liked. The way your words got tangled in your throat. I knew exactly what that felt like because I'd been feeling the same way since the end of camp.

"Wait, you guys have to kiss at the end of the show, right?" Kaylee gasped. "Oh, I bet Juniper *hates* that."

"Oh, you know." Teddy gave a nervous little laugh.

The room started spinning. I felt like I was in gym class that time that I got dared to press my forehead on the handle of a baseball bat and twirl around it in a merry-go-round of dizziness.

"She's not . . ." Kaylee clasped her hands below her chin. "She's not your *girlfriend*, is she?"

Lou turned and locked eyes with me. She had an expression on her face that I couldn't read. Maybe it was because my vision had gone blurry. My stomach turned, sweat ran down the back of my neck. I'd never felt more stupid in my entire life.

"Jack, are you all right?" Teddy said, noticing that I looked like a cracked egg simmering in a hot pan. I flinched as he said my name. "You look a little . . ."

But I didn't hear the end of what he said. All the anxiety of the day—the frosty bus ride with the cast, the skeptical stage manager, the silent treatment from my best friend, the girlfriend of the boy I liked—they all seemed to swirl together like toxic sludge in my stomach. All at once I felt it lurch through my body like a punch in the gut. I couldn't stop it from coming. I reached my hands up and covered my mouth, turning and sprinting across the floral carpeting. I was about to . . . *Oh no—*

Louisa

THE THREE OF US STOOD slightly stunned, staring down the hallway in the direction Jack had gone running.

"What just happened?" Teddy finally asked, hesitantly. "Did I say something wrong?"

"Poor guy," said Kaylee, shaking her head. "He looked like he was about to, you know, *hurl* . . ." She grimaced as she said the word.

"What should we do?" Teddy looked to me, visibly upset. "Should we go see if he's okay?"

I'm sure he expected me to have an immediate solution, being Jack's best friend. Of course neither he nor Kaylee realized that Jack and I weren't really speaking to each other, and I didn't want to make an already awkward moment even more awkward by telling them all about our fight the day before. And there was no way I was going to tell them what I strongly suspected: that Jack had gotten sick over the idea of Teddy having a girlfriend.

"Let's give him a minute," I suggested, figuring that such a plan would accomplish two things: give Jack some time to himself, which he probably needed, and give me some time to figure out how to proceed, since he and I were on such shaky ground. The truth was I did feel bad for Jack. Sure, we'd had a fight, but I was still sensitive to the fact that heartache had just been added to his list of problems. You know how it is with fights, though; they're like wells—easy to fall into, and nearly impossible to climb out.

"He said he was feeling carsick earlier," Teddy offered. "Maybe it's more serious than that?"

"I don't think so," I said, shaking my head. "I think he's probably just nervous about tomorrow."

"Sure, that's understandable." Kaylee nodded in support, then looked toward the ballroom.

"Should we go in and wait for him to come back?" she asked. "I want to make sure we get good seats."

I could tell Kaylee was anxious to get inside. As much as I would have liked to see Sierra Boggess perform, I also knew I wouldn't be able to concentrate while my heartsick friend was suffering alone in his hotel room.

"Sure, you go ahead," I said. "I think I'd better check on Jack."

"Okay, tell him I hope he feels better," Kaylee said. "You coming, Teddy?"

"Just a sec," Teddy replied, still concerned. Blowing air kisses, Kaylee pivoted away from us and headed through the double doors to the ballroom. I turned back to face Teddy, who kept looking down the corridor behind me as if Jack might suddenly reappear. I realized then that I could take advantage of this moment alone with Teddy to gain some information—information that could potentially make Jack's situation better—or at the very least, less confusing.

"Hey, listen," I began cautiously, "I don't know if Jack and I will make it to the concert, but will you save a seat for us anyway? Or—do you think you'd rather sit with Juniper?" I made sure to ask the question without a trace of teasing; nonetheless, Teddy's cheeks turned crimson. He looked down at the floor, took a deep breath, then locked eyes with mine.

"I don't want to sit with Juniper," he replied carefully. "I'd much rather sit with . . . you guys."

"Okay, great," I said, nodding, feeling fairly confident that I had the information I needed. "Hopefully we'll see you soon."

Once Teddy had disappeared into the ballroom, I dug my phone out of my pocket to text my mom.

ME: *CAN'T GO 2 CONCERT. HAVE 2 TALK 2 JACK ABOUT SOMETHING. WILL MEET U AFTER—BACK @ ROOM.*

I felt really weird as I walked down the hallway toward the elevators. On the surface, everything seemed normal. Soft jazz played from unseen speakers, and beige signs informed me where the conference rooms and fitness center were located. But there was nothing normal about mentally preparing myself for the conversation in which I told my best friend that I knew he was gay. There was nothing I could draw on in my life before this moment that would help, no comparisons I could make. I just hoped that whatever happened next would keep our friendship intact.

☆ ☆ ☆ ☆ ☆

Minutes later, my knuckles rapped softly on the door to Jack's room.

"It's me," I called, still clueless as to what I would actually say when he opened the door. In the elevator on the way up to his floor, I'd been overwhelmed by thoughts, but then an image emerged in my brain: the last day of Camp Curtain Up, when I caught Jack watching Teddy perform from the wings of the stage. He'd been so startled when I came up behind him, like he'd been ambushed. I had to be careful to not make him feel that way now. The current situation needed to be handled delicately.

Jack opened the door, his face drained of color.

"Sorry," he said, "I got really nauseous for some reason."

"Do you want me to get your mom?"

"No, it's okay," he said, smiling weakly. "I'm just a little shaky, but I'm fine." He paused, then asked, "You wanna come in?"

I stepped into the room, immediately noticing Jack's notebook open on his bed, filled with all his ideas and drawings.

"Still working?"

"Just reviewing some stuff," Jack said sheepishly.

"Don't worry—I'm not gonna make any more cuts." Jack shuffled sock-footed over to the bed and closed the notebook.

Watching him, I was suddenly overcome with nervousness; how in the world was I going to start this conversation?

"Um."

Jack turned to me, his face pale and expectant. "Yeah?"

I stood next to the desk, running my index finger along the edge of the leather-bound room service menu.

"So," I began, "I'm pretty sure that Juniper girl isn't Teddy's girlfriend."

I hoped Jack's face would offer a sign of relief, or even better, somehow let me know with just an expression that he understood what I was really talking about, but he quickly looked down at the floor.

"Okay," was all he said in response.

"He was really worried about you when you ran off," I said, now fiddling with the laminated card that asked you to reuse your towels. It was seemingly impossible to get through this without props.

"I'll text him and Kaylee, tell them I'm okay," Jack said, digging in his back pocket for his phone.

"Jack—" I took a step toward him.

"Let's forget about yesterday," he interrupted, letting his phone drop on the bed. "I didn't mean what I said about you only being mad 'cause it was your song. I was just—"

"And I didn't mean that we messed up our show," I rushed to add. "I think I was just feeling anxious . . ."

"Yeah, I hear that," Jack said, going a little green.

"But, Jack—" I began, then stopped short, all the words getting caught in my throat.

"What?"

There was no way Jack could know what I was about to say; perhaps an ambush was unavoidable. I cleared my throat and continued, "I think I know part of the reason why this whole Ghostlight thing has been so stressful for you."

"What do you mean?"

"I mean . . ."

As I hesitated, fearful of saying the wrong thing, Jack eyed me suspiciously. I knew I needed to say something, and soon; otherwise Jack might write me off as a complete lunatic. But what I finally blurted out didn't even come close to the eight hundred other things I'd considered saying.

"I like Tanner, okay?"

Jack looked at me, thoroughly confused. After a moment, though, he smirked.

"Yeah, I know, Lou," Jack said, amused. "That's been obvious since, like, February."

"But," I sputtered, "I'm telling you now! And it's been hard to tell you!"

For the first time since we'd arrived in Columbus, Jack allowed himself to laugh.

"I get it, Lou," he said. "But it's not a big deal. And it certainly hasn't been stressing me out. It's okay to like Tanner."

I started to laugh, too.

"Well, good!"

Even though I wasn't really there to talk about Tanner, I still felt a rush of relief as I confessed my feelings out loud. It didn't mean I was going to do anything about them, but allowing myself to talk about them made me feel so much better. I knew it was now my turn to offer Jack that same relief.

From somewhere deep inside I found the courage to look him straight in the eye.

"So, Jack?"

"Yeah?"

"It's also okay to like Teddy."

Jack's look of surprise quickly gave way to panic, and I watched his chest rise and fall as his breathing quickened.

"I haven't said anything because I wasn't sure," I said hurriedly, "but then when you ran off just now . . ."

"Did you say anything to Teddy?" Jack asked, the panic rising in his voice.

"No, I would never," I assured him. "But just so you know, he *definitely* wanted to sit with you."

A prolonged silence filled the room as Jack slowly sat down on the edge of his bed and turned his face away from me while I continued to stand awkwardly by the desk. Suddenly his hands flew to his eyes, tears catching him by surprise.

"Sorry," he murmured.

"Don't be sorry," I said, debating whether to go to him or stay put. "I'm sorry you felt like you couldn't talk to me about it."

"It's not like I've been sure myself," Jack said after a moment, wiping his cheeks with the back of his hand. "I'm still not *really* sure . . . I mean, I just know that I like Teddy . . . Though he might not, you know . . ."

"I'm pretty sure he does," I ventured, causing Jack to sit up straighter.

"Really?" He sniffed.

"Well, it was kind of obvious that last night at camp . . ."

Jack squirmed the way I did when he teased me about Tanner.

"Oh, *jeez* . . ."

"Keeping a secret is tough," I said, finally joining him on the edge of the bed. We sat side by side, not saying anything, for what seemed like a long time. Finally, Jack turned to me, his eyes rimmed with red.

"You know what else is tough? Knowing that our show sucks."

"No!"

As much as I'd wanted to accuse him of that very thing yesterday, now all I wanted to do was assure him otherwise.

"It doesn't. It's just different. You took a risk and that's super brave."

"I just wanted us to win." He sighed. "I know how much you wanted to win."

"I did," I admitted, "but honestly—I don't even care anymore. I mean, I care about the show, but who cares about winning? Everyone else here is having such a great time—"

"—and we're miserable!" Jack interjected, making us both start to laugh again. It was true—Kaylee and Teddy had promised an amazing weekend filled with like-minded theater nerds, and here we were having a serious life moment in a dark, lonely hotel room while everyone else was geeking out over some belting Broadway diva on the first floor.

"Do you want to go back downstairs?" I asked. "I bet we could still catch the last bit of the concert."

"I don't think I could deal with seeing Teddy right now," Jack said, shaking his head. "I'd be too self-conscious with both of you there."

I understood what he meant, imagining the next time I'd be with Tanner and Jack at the same time. So embarrassing.

"What if we just raid the vending machine, then?" I suggested. Jack's eyes lit up. Having a health nut for a mom, meant he rarely got to eat junk food.

"Yes!" he exclaimed, reaching for his nightstand

and scraping loose change into his hand. "I'm finally hungry!" We jumped up and headed toward the door, but as Jack put his hand on the doorknob, he paused.

"For the record," he said, twisting his torso to look at me. "Teddy's not the main reason I wanted to do Ghostlight."

"I know," I said, smiling mischievously. "But it's so much more fun to pretend that it is."

"Oh no, I'll never hear the end of it, will I?" Jack said, rolling his eyes in mock despair.

As he opened the door I whispered in his ear, "Remember that time you made me give up *Sound of Music* so you could be with your boyfriend?"

Without missing a beat, he shot back, "Remember that time you gave up *Sound of Music* so you could be with *your* boyfriend?!" And with that, Jack took off running down the hall with me close on his heels, both of us shrieking with laughter.

Jack

I SLEPT MORE SOUNDLY THAT night than I had in months. I wasn't sure if it was the mountain of fluffy hotel pillows or the mountain of vending-machine candy bars Lou and I had devoured while watching late-night cable, but the mattress absorbed my body like quicksand, and I woke up feeling new.

Talking with Lou and finally opening up about Teddy with another person felt like taking off a backpack that had been filled with rocks. I'd thought that admitting that I liked Teddy—acknowledging that I was different—would make me feel alone. But I'd clearly underestimated my best friend. And if what she thought about Teddy was true, I had not one, but two reasons to feel like I belonged.

Of course, not *everything* was in its right place. I still had to direct a show that I wasn't even sure I believed in, with a cast of friends who felt like I'd let them down. While I got ready to face the day—I must've changed T-shirts ten times—I noticed the competition schedule resting on my bedside table. We were set to present *The Fantasticks* at one thirty that afternoon, which meant that we had to be on deck, ready to perform, by one o'clock. All at once I knew what had to be done. I'd never been good at math, but I knew enough to calculate that there was still time to fix what I'd so thoroughly messed up.

"Mom," I called, snatching a room key off the dresser. "I have to go find my cast."

"You sure you don't want to wait for me?" she asked from the bathroom, drying her hair with a fluffy Marriott towel.

"No, this is an emergency. I'll text you when I find them."

I charged down to breakfast without even brushing my teeth. I bypassed the elevator for the stairs, jumping down two steps at a time. I stormed through the lobby, passing buffets of fruit salad and kids making a mess at the Belgian waffle maker. Finally, I spied a table with some familiar faces in the back of the restaurant.

"You guys," I gasped, trying to catch my breath as I collapsed into their booth.

Lou and Jenny halted their conversation, and Tanner looked up from the pancakes that he was currently drowning in syrup.

"We need to get everyone together," I said frantically. "I have an idea."

☆☆☆☆☆

"You want to do *what?*" Jenny blurted, almost spitting an entire mouthful of grapefruit juice into my face. I looked around the table at my cast, who were all in various states of dress, some still wearing slippers and pajama bottoms.

I could hear Belinda's bus-ride advice playing through my head: *"Go with your gut and hope for the best."*

"I want to change the show back to what it was before," I exclaimed. "Back to when we enjoyed rehearsing and I'd never spoken the words *concept* or *reality TV*."

Eight pairs of eyes stared back at me in disbelief. I knew that what I was asking was crazy, but I also knew that it was crazy to perform a show that nobody—cast, crew, or director—really believed in.

"But how?" Raj interjected. "We perform in, what? Four hours?"

"Well, if you think about it, that's almost two whole after-school rehearsals," I reasoned. "Think of how much we were able to do back in Shaker Heights. It can't be that hard to strip away all the nonsense and get back to what was actually working."

My cast still looked skeptical.

"Come on, guys!" Belinda said, throwing down her English muffin. "Yesterday we were all such mopes, and now our director is giving us the opportunity to turn this all around."

Belinda rose from the table, adopting a strong stance, a marmalade-covered butter knife still in her hand.

"We all signed up to do a Jack Goodrich show, and now he's giving us the chance to do something great," she continued in a rousing voice strangely reminiscent of Alice Ripley's Tony Awards acceptance speech for *Next to Normal*. "Just think of the story we'll be able to tell!"

The cast's heads turned slightly, trying to catch glimpses of anyone who might be feeling the same way.

"I say we do it!" Belinda cheered, raising her butter knife into the air. "Who's with me?"

☆ ☆ ☆ ☆ ☆

"I found us a conference room!" my mom cheered, flying down triumphantly to our table the second I texted her with the big news.

Together, our cast surged through the hotel with a newfound determination, like we were student soldiers boarding the barricade in *Les Misérables*. Everywhere we looked we saw groups of kids nervously heading to their own presentations—middle-schoolers dressed as orphans and greasers and dancing silverware. As we turned a corner on the second floor, I heard a voice call my name from the throng of passing students, then a hand on my wrist, spinning me around.

It was Teddy.

"Are you okay, buddy?" he said, pulling us out of the traffic jam of students. "You seemed pretty far gone last night."

"Yeah, I'm all right," I replied. "It was this stupid . . . stomach thing. I'm much better now."

"That's good to hear," he said sympathetically. "I was worried about you."

We just stood there for a few seconds. I could still feel the spot on my arm where he'd grabbed me with his hand, like a little spark on the hairs of my wrist. But I reluctantly shifted my gaze to the group of my friends disappearing down the hallway without me.

"Thanks for thinking of me, Teddy," I said, snapping out of the moment and grabbing him by the shoulders. "And I'd love to continue this conversation, but right now, I have to go save my show!"

☆ ☆ ☆ ☆ ☆

The next four hours were the craziest of my life: crazier than lines at Cedar Point the weekend their new roller coaster opened; crazier than Shubert Alley the weekend of the Broadway Flea Market; crazier than the final callbacks for *A Christmas Story*, where forty kids piled into a room and learned the entire dance break to "You'll Shoot Your Eye Out" in just twenty minutes.

The conference room was only half the size of the actual stage, and it was filled with tables, chairs, and decorative plastic plants, but even in the crowded space, the show started to improve almost immediately after we resurrected the original script that I'd "modernized" into critical condition. I was amazed at how quickly the old moments came back to us, and whenever we drew a blank, Belinda, our new MVP, jumped in to remind us of our old blocking. (It turns out that she'd taken detailed descriptions of my staging, perhaps hoping that one day we'd reach this conclusion on our own.) My mom was able to run down a copy of our original cues to the festival stage manager just as the first school was loading in to perform. Laughter filled the room and smiles returned to our faces as we pieced together the magic we'd created in those first few weeks. And slowly, the idea of performing some slick, perfect presentation didn't seem to matter all that much. We were having fun again—and that was the most that I could ask from any cast.

Just as we finished restaging the bows, a woman wearing a "Ghostlight Staff" T-shirt popped her head into the room. "Shaker Heights Middle School, you're on deck!"

The butterflies returned to my stomach the second we arrived at the ballroom, just like they had the day before—but this time it wasn't because I was dreading what was waiting inside.

"Okay, guys," I said to my cast, now circled up and holding hands as I gave my final pep talk. "I know that what I'm asking you to do is crazy. I know that in a perfect world, we'd have another month to rehearse this version."

"Or, you know, like, a time machine." Tanner laughed.

"Fair enough." I smiled. "But I wouldn't have sprung this on you if I wasn't sure that you guys could pull it off."

I looked around the circle at my friends, remembering back to that Sunday morning in September when we'd all first gathered in the auditorium. It was hard to believe that with everything that had happened, these eight actors were still willing to put their trust in me.

"I know it's going to feel a little bit like you've been shot out of a cannon," I continued. "But if you just focus on telling the story, you can't go wrong. Be honest, listen to your fellow actors, and most importantly"—I sighed, feeling a tightness growing in my throat—"just go out there and have fun."

I watched my team disappear into the wings, and soon it was only Belinda and me, totally helpless to whatever might happen next.

"My mom saved me a seat, but I don't think I can sit in the audience," I confessed, looking up at her. "I'm too anxious."

"Oh, honey, I'm the same way," she agreed. "Come stand in the back with me. We can pace nervously together."

As the lights dimmed, I spotted two familiar figures taking a seat in the second row. It was Kaylee and Teddy! I'd thought for sure they would be preparing for their own presentations. I couldn't tell if I was more excited to see their faces or terrified that they might be embarrassed by what was about to emerge from behind the curtain.

Our presentation began with Mr. Hennessy playing the jingly overture to the show. The first person to enter was Jenny, wearing a race-car-red leotard and a ballet skirt, springing from the wings in a split-leap *jeté* that made half the audience gasp in amazement. She proceeded to decorate the stage, arranging chairs between pirouettes and pulling costumes out of the trunk with flourishes and turns. I realized now how criminal it was to strap a camera on the shoulder of this beautiful ballerina and how lucky we were to see someone dance their own choreography.

Tanner was the first to sing, drawing us in with the gorgeous melody of "Try to Remember" just like he had his first day of rehearsal. Sebastian brought charisma to the poetic love song "Metaphor," and Lou dazzled, popping out silvery high notes in her solo, "Much More." (Now that she didn't have to spend the final verse pretending to choose the perfect photo filter, her voice was able to soar.)

Of course, not everything was perfect. Some of the blocking was forgotten, and the occasional line was dropped. Tanner was probably the biggest offender, sometimes paraphrasing dialogue and even once reverting back to the old, *concept* version. In the speech where the two lovers meet in the forest, he was supposed to say "And love was sweeter than the berries," but instead decreed, "And love was sweeter than Ben and Jerry's." Immediately he noticed his mistake and spent the rest of the monologue trying to stifle his own laughter. Sebastian got the giggles, too, and even Lou, the most professional of them all, had to turn upstage to keep from breaking character. Still, I couldn't be mad; the sight of my cast enjoying themselves, even because of a mistake, was more gratifying than the most sincere performance of *The Fantasticks: The Reality Show* ever could be.

In the Henry and Mortimer scene, Raj recited his Shakespeare lines with the polish of an actor three times his age—I couldn't believe I'd ever thought it was a good idea to cut them. And during Mortimer's fake death scene, Radhika committed so thoroughly that she almost toppled off the stage. Luckily, Tanner was there to catch her, his soccer-goalie reflexes coming in handy.

Sarah and Esther were the only two actors a little sad to see the modern version go—they loved getting to play the mothers like rich New Jersey housewives. In the end, I decided to let them stick with the characterizations, and thank goodness I did. The audience roared with laughter as they tripped across the stage in tall stiletto heels, pretending to pull each other's hair and throw wineglasses full of water in each other's faces.

Halfway through the presentation, I stopped counting how many small mistakes were being made. If the people in the audience even noticed, their applause and laughter seemed to suggest that they didn't mind. What was most clear was that everyone was having a great time.

The one scene where everything came together exactly as rehearsed was when Lou and Sebastian entered the stage to perform "Soon It's Gonna Rain." They sang the tune better than I'd ever heard, infused with the kind of joy that only comes from being reunited with something sorely missed. In the final verse, where Jenny sprinkled the blue tissue paper from above, the audience was so quiet, you could hear the tiny shreds of "rain" falling gently on the stage.

The most shocking moment came toward the end of the presentation, when Tanner entered for the abduction scene. As a director, I'd made it a theme that whenever El Gallo was playing the kidnapper, he would tie a red scarf around his neck and take it off when he was addressing us as the narrator. But this time, Tanner had forgotten his scarf. I could tell Jenny noticed, too, but I could have never anticipated what happened next. With only moments to spare, Jenny grabbed ahold of her silk ballet skirt and pulled hard, tearing off a ribbon of red cloth. She ran over to Tanner and tied it around his neck before dashing offstage. I turned to Belinda in shock. She was just as surprised as me; if there was one thing Jenny cared more about than her dancing, it was her fashion.

I was so exhilarated, I barely noticed that thirty minutes had flown by. Before I knew it, Mr. Hennessy was playing the intricate arpeggios of the finale as our cast trilled their final *Love! Love!* chorus. I could feel my eyes beginning to well up with tears. It was imperfect and under-rehearsed, probably even a little bit sloppy, but not a single person in the audience could deny the passion radiating from the stage. As the lights blacked out, an explosion of applause erupted from the students and parents surrounding us. My palms stung as I clapped louder than I ever had in my life, so proud of everything we'd done.

And in that moment, I became suddenly struck with a realization—our journey with the show wasn't so different than that of the two lovers in *The Fantasticks*. We'd set out in search of some shinier, fantasy world only to return home, battered and bruised, realizing the answers were right there in our own backyards.

Louisa

I STOOD IN THE DARKNESS, stunned. Our presentation had been nowhere near perfect, with lots of goofy mistakes, uneven pacing, and a wild energy that no doubt came from a super-intense four-hour emergency rehearsal that ended minutes before our call time. But the applause now erupting around us was unmistakable in its enthusiasm. Loud cheers and high-pitched whistles bounced off the walls, confirming that despite our gaffes, we'd miraculously pulled it off. In anticipation of the lights coming back up, my castmates and I fumbled for one another's hands so that we'd be in position for our curtain call. I felt Tanner's hand reach for mine, and as the lights hit our faces, he gripped it so tightly, I thought my fingers might break.

"I guess we did okay!" he shouted over the noise of the crowd. I nodded, still in a state of disbelief. We bowed twice, and as we were about to walk off the stage I caught Jack's silhouette in the back of the ballroom, jumping up and down and pumping his arms in the air. *Yep*, I thought, *I guess we did okay.*

We skipped off the stage, already laughing about all the things that had gone wrong and gushing with praise for what had gone right:

"Oh my God, sorry I was late for that entrance—I was looking for my camera and then forgot I didn't need it anymore!"

"Jenny, your dance was incredible!"

"Radhika—you were hilarious!"

"You mean when I almost fell off the stage?"

"But Tanner totally saved you—it was amazing!"

"Yeah, and you should do stand-up, Tanner—how'd you come up with those lines?"

"I don't know, I can't remember anything I said!"

"Oh, Sebastian and Lou—you guys almost made me cry!"

We could have gone on like that for hours, probably, but Trish the technical director was having none of it.

"Please clear the area," she barked. "The next school needs access to the stage to get their set in place."

We responded with a chorus of *oopses* and *sorrys*, then scampered toward the back of the ballroom. On our way to the exit, a uniform line of kids dressed in immaculate costumes began to pass us on their way to the stage. Cavendish was up next.

"Lou, you guys were *great*!" Teddy, dressed in a crisp gray suit, a Bluetooth hooked over his right ear, jumped out of the line to give me a hug. We had to flatten ourselves against the wall to let our castmates pass in either direction.

"I couldn't watch your whole presentation 'cause I had to go to our preshow pep-talk thing, but I thought it was so good," he said. "Jack did an amazing job." I smiled, thinking how pleased Jack would be to hear that.

"I thought you guys were doing a modern thing with it, though?" Teddy asked. "What made Jack change his mind?" I worked hard at keeping a straight face, thinking how much drama the complete and honest answer to his question entailed.

"It's a long story, Teddy," I said, "But I'm sure Jack will fill you in at some point."

"Okay! Can't wait!" he called over his shoulder as he ran to catch up with his cast.

"Break a leg!" I called back.

Out in the hallway, a euphoric Jack and Belinda were engulfed in a group hug, while all the parent chaperones took photos and videos with their phones. I gave my mom a quick squeeze ("You sparkled up there, Lulu!" she whispered into my hair), then rejoined my friends as the swirl of congratulations turned into an animated interrogation of Jack and Belinda as everyone demanded to know how the show *really* went.

"I mean, so much went wrong, but then they were, like, *crazy* afterwards," said Jenny, still buzzing with adrenaline.

"Be honest—was it *actually* good," asked Esther, "or is everyone just really nice here?"

Jack laughed.

"You guys were awesome, seriously," he gushed. "Your energy was so great, it was contagious—"

"And that's what made everyone love you,"

Belinda chimed in, beaming, "and you all worked together to tell a great story. The mistakes . . ." She flicked her hand in the air as if shooing away a fly.

"The mistakes didn't matter at all," confirmed Jack, catching my eye. "I'm so proud of you guys. Thank you for being so amazing."

"Thank *you*!" I cheered, setting off a rapid-fire round of more *thank yous* from everyone else.

"Shh!" We looked over to see a stern attendant hissing at us, his bald head poking through one of the slightly opened ballroom doors. "The next school is about to perform!"

As everyone continued to giggle quietly, Jack and I exchanged a meaningful look. We needed to head back inside to watch Cavendish.

"Excuse us," I said to the group, "we're gonna check out the competition."

☆ ☆ ☆ ☆ ☆

Back inside, the energy of the room had cranked up a notch. It made sense—the reigning champion of Ghostlight was about to perform; of course expectations were running high. Jack and I found two aisle seats in the sixth row, and just as we were about to sit down:

"I think they should get points off for having such a long title."

We turned to see Tanner standing next to us, the red swath of cloth from Jenny's ballet skirt still draped around his neck. He stared scornfully at the stage. Behind him stood Jenny, and behind her stood the rest of our cast, all looking for seats.

"I mean, c'mon," Tanner continued, "*How to Succeed in Whatever Without Really Doing Whatever*? Who has time to say all that?"

"What are you guys doing in here?" I asked, genuinely surprised to see everyone. I assumed now that their work was done that they'd have gone off to find the indoor pool or retreat to their hotel rooms to watch movies. Was it possible that they were all embracing their inner MTNs?

"Whoa, *'scuse us*," Tanner said playfully, "is this, like, special Jack and Lou time?"

"N-no, of course not," I sputtered, embarrassed. "You guys should totally stay—if you want to."

"Then move over," ordered Tanner, and Jack and I complied by scooting over one seat to the right, making room for Tanner on my left. As he sat down, I felt Jack's elbow poking me in the ribs, and I elbowed him back so hard that he let out an "Oof!"

Jenny, finding a seat directly behind me and Jack, leaned in between us.

"Hey, look," she said, pointing to the stage, where the Cavendish kids were setting up their flat-screen TVs and contemporary rolling desk chairs, "they have a 'concept.'" She said it in such a deadpan way that we all started to giggle. Thank goodness we were already able to find humor in what we'd been through these past few weeks.

"Guys, quiet," Tanner whispered with mock sternness. "*How to Do All the Stuff Without Doing Any Stuff* is starting."

☆ ☆ ☆ ☆ ☆

Everything we'd heard about Cavendish was true. Their sets were fancier, their costumes sleeker, their props way more expensive. The actors were slick, polished, and professional, enunciating each word with perfect diction and executing each dance move with a sharpness that only came from hours and hours of rehearsal. Unlike our presentation, it was impossible to spot any mistakes. But the best part of the Cavendish presentation had nothing to do with its fancy trappings or its perfect execution. The best part, by far, was watching Jack watch

Teddy, who shone as J. Pierpont Finch. Every time Teddy sang, Jack would lean forward in his chair and rest his elbows on his knees, listening intently to each note. Whenever Teddy landed a laugh with the audience, Jack's grin practically took over his entire face. And when the lights came down and the audience exploded even louder than it had exploded for us, the biggest cheers of all came from Jack.

"Wooo-hoooo!" he screamed, prompting Tanner to turn to me, confused.

"Aren't we supposed to, like, hate them?" he asked over the applause.

"No!" I shouted back. "The lead guy is our good friend from camp!"

"Oh, okay," Tanner replied. I could tell he was still confused as he reluctantly clapped his hands together.

"Whew!" Jack said once the applause had subsided. "It's always great when you don't have to lie to someone after a show. I can honestly tell Teddy that he was incredible."

"You sure can—he was pretty perfect," I agreed, then asked, somewhat cautiously, "Can you *also* honestly say that you're still glad we did our old version of *The Fantasticks* after seeing Cavendish perform?"

Jack paused, then smiled.

"I can," he said proudly. "I mean, all their modern stuff was really cool, but sticking with the traditional version was definitely better for us."

"I totally agree," Jenny said emphatically, inserting herself into our conversation, "their show worked much better with a modern twist. Ours . . ." She made a face like she was sucking on a lemon wedge. Jack and I exchanged a look. *All right, Jenny, point taken.*

"Who's up next?" Tanner asked.

"Our friend Kaylee's school," Jack replied.

"Jeez—do you guys have friends from *every* school?"

"No, only from Cavendish Prep and Rustin Middle," Jack said with a smile.

"They're doing a show called *Once on This Island*," I added.

"Still too long," Tanner grunted, cracking his knuckles.

Just then Kaylee and the rest of her cast came filing in, passing the Cavendish kids, who were now filing out.

I watched as Kaylee grabbed Teddy to give him a congratulatory hug, much like the one Teddy had given me after our presentation.

"It's so weird here," I heard Tanner remark. He had followed my gaze over to where my friends chatted excitedly.

"We would never do that with our competition before a soccer game," he said, shaking his head in wonder.

"Well, it's different in theater," I replied, feeling a rush of pride and joy as I thought about what I'd just said. It *was* different in theater. Sure, the next Ghostlight champion would be named tomorrow, but . . .

"The winning and losing part isn't what makes this special," I continued, thinking back to the last night of Camp Curtain Up, when Kaylee and Teddy had first told me and Jack about Ghostlight and what it was that made them love it so much. The chance to celebrate their shared love of doing theater with other kids was what got them so excited to return. And it's why they wanted us to be here, too.

"You're saying you don't care if we lose?" Tanner asked, still skeptical.

"I'm saying it's not as important as being part of something," I said as I watched my two incredibly talented friends from two completely different schools exchange enthusiastic, heartfelt hugs. We were all here for each other—that was the real prize.

Tanner chuckled softly.

"Okay," he said, "I guess that's sorta cool."

A few minutes later, after Kaylee and her castmates had arranged their simple set pieces on the stage, the lights dimmed once again. *Once on This Island*'s prologue began:

"There is an island where rivers run deep

Where the sea sparkling in the sun earns it

The name 'Jewel of the Antilles'. . ."

The pulsing rhythm of the musical introduction sent a chill racing up my spine. A split second later I realized that the spinal jolt had actually nothing to do with the music; it was because Tanner's hand was suddenly resting halfway on top of mine. I froze, keeping completely still, as I wondered whether the placement of his hand was some kind of accident, and whether anyone (namely Jack or Jenny) had noticed. There was a chance Tanner didn't even know we were touching.

But then, after a few moments, he lifted his fingers and gently curled them around mine. I instantly had two thoughts: the first, that there was nothing accidental about intertwined fingers; the second, how different this hand-holding was from when Tanner almost crushed my fingers during the curtain call. With what felt like a great deal of courage, I pressed the tips of my fingers into his hand. He turned his head in my direction to flash the Grin, which prompted my stomach to flip over about twenty times. On the other side of me I felt Jack's elbow digging into my ribs once again, followed moments later by Jenny pulling on the waistband of my skirt from her seat behind me. *Guess they noticed.* But as I sat there watching Kaylee and her classmates deliver a stunning performance of *Once on This Island*, I didn't feel embarrassed. I just felt happy.

Playing Ti Moune, Kaylee sang that she was *"waiting for life to begin,"* yearning for opportunity and adventure. I realized that, at least in this moment, I wasn't waiting for anything. My life—the life I dreamed of living—had most certainly begun.

Jack

"AND THE WINNER OF THE Ghostlight Festival is . . ."

My grip tightened around Lou's shoulders as the announcer's voice echoed through the event center. The memories from the previous two days all swirled together in my head like a kaleidoscope. The only sound that could be heard was the tearing of envelope paper and the sounds of a thousand hearts beating in unison.

"Rustin Middle School, for *Once on This Island*!"

A seismic wave of screams and cheers swept the auditorium as the entire audience leaped to its feet. Of course Rustin Middle School won!

The second Kaylee opened her mouth to sing the first notes of Ahrens and Flaherty's enchanting, soulful score, everyone in the audience realized the contest was over. While *Once on This Island* didn't have the slickness of Cavendish's *How to Succeed* or the improvised comedy of our *The Fantasticks*, the simple beauty of their stripped-down performance—plus Kaylee's devastating pipes—made Rustin a shoo-in for first place. In the end, it didn't matter how cutting-edge a concept was, or how much money was spent on sets and costumes. The school that simply told the story the best was the one that took home the trophy.

Lou and I screamed ourselves hoarse as the Rustin Middle School team swarmed the stage, their faces streaked with tears as they passed the giant trophy down to our friend and newly crowned Queen of Ghostlight, Kaylee Cooper.

As for Cavendish? They placed second, collecting high points in creativity and production elements. As for Shaker Heights Middle School . . . we came in eighth. It was still a pretty amazing feat for a school that had never even competed before—and whose entire show had been rebuilt in the span of an afternoon.

Once the commotion finally ended, representatives from each of the top ten teams joined Rustin Middle School on the stage to collect our plaques. Even over all the applause, I could hear the sound of Teddy whistling with his fingers as I took a self-conscious bow.

As the cheering subsided, the cast of *Once on This Island* started a celebratory and impromptu a cappella version of "Why We Tell the Story." The rest of us joined in with gusto.

"Hope is why we tell the story,
Faith is why we tell the story,
You are why we tell the story."

☆ ☆ ☆ ☆ ☆

"I feel like I'm dreaming," Kaylee said, hugging Lou around the waist.

The Four Musketeers had gathered in the lobby following the awards ceremony, savoring our final moments together while our parents and chaperones settled bills, returned room keys, and tried to track down Tanner, who had insisted on bouncing on his hotel bed one last time.

"Excuse me—you're the girl who played Ti Moune, right?" a nearby girl asked shyly, her group approaching us nervously. "Can we take a selfie with you?"

"Are you for real?" Kaylee laughed. "Of course!"

Lou, Teddy, and I stepped out of the way as Kaylee leaned in and smiled alongside the pack of grinning strangers (the first of many moments in the spotlight for Kaylee, if I may be so bold).

"Thank you so much!" the shortest girl said nervously. "You are going to be so famous one day!"

"Omigosh," Kaylee gasped, still clearly in shock from her newfound fame. "Thank you so much!"

"Thank YOU!" the girl's friends cheered before they skipped off, fired up from having a picture with the rising star of Ghostlight.

"Next year we're going to need to get you a security detail," Teddy whispered with a grin, once the kids were out of earshot.

Following our performances last night, Teddy and I finally got to spend the time together that had motivated me to come to Ghostlight in the first place. We brushed elbows at dinner, filling our spoons with gross things for him to eat in his newest game: Rodgers and Hammerstein Sludge Bucket. We laughed as we rode the escalator up and down with Lou and Kaylee until the hotel's overnight manager demanded that we went to bed. But we still hadn't had a chance to talk just the two of us. Even at the dance mixer, where I promised myself that I'd say something, the music was too loud and the dance floor too crowded to have a serious conversation. Now I found myself standing with my suitcase, ready to head back to life in Shaker Heights, and I still hadn't uttered a word about how much he meant to me.

"Oh no," Kaylee said, looking out the giant glass doors of the Marriott. "My bus just pulled up in the driveway. I think it's that time."

The Musketeers groaned, pulling her in for one last giant hug, whispering words of congratulations and promises to stay in touch. We watched her disappear into the November daylight, a champion leaving the ring in victory.

"When does the Cavendish bus leave?" I asked Teddy.

"Not for another hour," he replied. "But I came down anyway. I didn't want to miss saying good-bye to you guys."

"Aw, you're the best," Lou said, hugging him around the waist.

We compared travel times and road-trip snacks

that we'd bought from the gift shop. We talked about our hometowns and the ways we'd spend the last few weeks of autumn. We swapped Ghostlight memories and hopes for our next starring roles, and before we knew it, our moms were calling for us from across the lobby.

"Jack and Lou!" Mrs. Benning said. "Time to get on the bus!"

"Ugh. We have to go." Lou frowned. "Thank you so much for convincing us to do Ghostlight," she said, pulling Teddy in for a hug.

"You promise you don't regret not doing *Sound of Music*?" he asked, hugging her tight.

"I wouldn't trade this weekend," she said, her eyes beginning to fill with her token good-bye tears, "for anything. I'll see you next summer!"

Lou wiped her face with her sleeve and grabbed ahold of her rolling suitcase. As she turned to leave, she gave me an encouraging nod, both of us knowing that if I was going to say something to Teddy, now would be my last shot. I looked back to Teddy, whose hands were in his pockets. He rocked slightly back and forth on his feet. I couldn't help but be reminded of Camp Curtain Up, that afternoon in August where we stood just like this, neither of us quite knowing how to say good-bye.

"Lou's totally right," I said finally. "This weekend was pretty incredible."

"Even the part where you puked your guts out?" he asked, giving my arm a little punch.

"Well, okay, not everything." I laughed.

I looked down at my shoes and took in a deep breath. *Now or never*, the voice echoed in my head. *Now or never.*

"But, Teddy." I looked him straight in the face. "I did like all the parts that I got to spend with you."

I watched as the words played through his mind, his eyes flickering slightly with recognition.

"Aw, come here," he said, wrapping his arms around me.

The hardest part was over, I told myself, resting my chin on his shoulder. *Whatever happens now is out of my control.*

"Maybe you can come visit us on winter break or something?" I said, pulling out of the hug and reaching down for my duffel bag.

"Yeah, maybe." He smiled. "I'd like that."

"Jack!" I heard my mom call again. I could see my cast through the big glass windows, boarding our yellow school bus.

"Okay," I said, slinging the strap over my shoulder. "I'll see ya."

"Bye, Jack." He nodded and gave me that unforgettable crooked smile.

I turned and walked to the exit. My shoulders dropped an inch, finally unloading the weight that came from having to guard a secret. Sure, I hadn't told him how many times a day he crossed my mind, or how I would replay our weekend in my head the entire bus ride back to Shaker Heights, but I had been brave enough to show him a little bit of what was going on in my heart, and for that, I had no regrets. I took one last look over my shoulder as I pushed through the revolving doors, Teddy's hand raising slowly, giving a little wave as he watched the wheel of glass return me safely to the reality of eighth grade.

A wall of sadness hit the second my foot stepped onto the bus, but it was different from what I'd felt on the drive down. It wasn't the worry of ruining a perfectly good show, or the anger of being in a fight with my best friend. It felt more like a tugging, an acknowledgment that things were probably going to be different now. My final scene with Teddy hadn't ended like it would have if we were characters in *The Fantasticks*, but I still had a feeling that everything was going to be okay.

My mood brightened ever so slightly as I walked up the aisle, passing the fond faces of my cast, past Raj and Radhika, who flashed me their twin grins, past Sebastian, who raised his hand for a fist bump, past Sarah and Esther and Jenny and Belinda, all smiling and congratulating me once again.

"Jack," a voice called from the back of the bus. "Come sit with us."

The voice belonged to Lou, who to my delight was wedged into a row with none other than Tanner Falzone. The only thing separating them was our Top Ten plaque, sandwiched between their blue jeans.

"We saved you a spot," Tanner said, reaching across the aisle and pulling his backpack off a vacant row. I stole a quick glance with Lou as I slid into my seat.

How did it go? her eyes asked.

I'll tell you later, my shoulders shrugged back.

For now, I was content with sitting back and watching my friend share a seat with her crush. I couldn't believe that after six months of enduring

Tanner's tireless flirting, she'd finally given in and allowed herself to like him back. And while I was over the moon, I couldn't help but feel a tiny sting of jealousy, knowing that I wanted those same things with Teddy.

Just as the engine of our bus rumbled to life, I felt my phone vibrate in my pocket. I fished it out and read the notification on my screen

"New Message from Teddy Waverly."

I swiped my finger, expecting a goofy selfie.

Hey buddy, the text read. *I realized I never really got to gush about how awesome The Fantasticks was! Stripping it down like that was so smart—you made our How to Succeed look so overdone. Haha. Lou was perfectly cast and as for the direction . . . is it lame to say it was fantastic? ;-)*

A huge smile spread across my face.

But mostly . . . the next text bubble read. *Mostly I'm sorry I didn't get to spend more time with you. Everyone who saw your show knows what an amazing director you are . . . but what's even more amazing is how you make me feel when I'm with you.*

The bottom of his text was signed with two

tiny symbols. Two simple characters that on their own meant little, but when put together made my eighth-grade existence burst open wide with possibilities.

<3

I looked around the crowded bus. Our driver, Larry, was turning his wheel, getting ready to pull out of the parking lot.

"WAIT!" I shouted, standing up in our row.

Larry screeched the brakes as every head on board turned back to look at me.

"What?" Belinda said, looking concerned.

"I forgot . . . ," I muttered, looking around the bus. "I forgot . . ." My eyes landing on Tanner and Lou. "I forgot our Top Ten plaque! I think I left it on the desk in the lobby."

Tanner reached underneath Lou's arm, "No, Jack, it's right—"

Lou cut him off, elbowing him in the side. "That's . . . right!" Lou jumped in, sliding the plaque under her leg. "That's right! I saw you leave it on the desk!"

"Oh, riiight." Tanner nodded slowly. "Yes . . . we can't *leave* . . . without our *plaque*," he said, overemphasizing the sound of worry in his voice.

"Okay," Belinda clipped. "Well, run back in and get it, Jack! We'll wait here."

"Totally!" I said, scrambling to the front of the bus. "I will be *so quick*!"

I leaped down the stairs of the bus and dashed up to the entrance of the hotel. I pushed through the revolving doors, my heart pounding like a drum. I sprinted through the lobby, a wave of instant relief crashing over me as my eyes landed on Teddy, who was thankfully still waiting, staring down at his phone.

"I like how I feel when I'm with you, too!" I blurted out.

Teddy looked up from his phone, a mixture of surprise and excitement spreading across his face.

"You do?" he said meekly.

"Yes," I breathed. "A lot, actually."

Teddy looked around the lobby, clearly startled by the spontaneity of my declaration. "Well . . . good," he said finally. "Me too."

"Yeah, I've felt that way since camp," I continued. "I just didn't know if I should tell you or if you even felt . . ." I shook my head. ". . . that way."

"Well, I'm glad you came back," Teddy said. "If you didn't reply to that text, I was pretty sure

I was going to have a heart attack." His face broke out into a wide grin.

"Don't do that," I said, kicking his shoe.

For a second we just stood there, laughing awkwardly, afraid to break eye contact. The whole thing began to seem ridiculous in hindsight—the hours I'd spent worrying, the negative thoughts playing through my head on loop, all that time unaware there was someone out there thinking those same things about me.

"Argh!" I growled. "I wish I could stay and tell you everything, but I *really* need to go."

"Yeah, yeah, don't miss your bus, stinker."

"Okay." I grinned. "Bye, Teddy."

I turned to walk away but felt a hand on my shoulder. This time, it was Teddy's turn to be spontaneous. He spun me around, placed his hand on the back of my head, and leaned in, gently touching his lips to mine. They felt soft and kind of warm, not wet and heavy like the kisses I'd seen in cheesy movies. As he pulled away, I could feel a breath of warm air exhale through his nose.

"I'm sorry," he said, blushing from his chin to his forehead. "I hope that was okay."

"It was," I replied, feeling a little light-headed.

"I'm . . ." I stammered. "I'm really glad I came back."

"Me too." Teddy giggled. "And for what it's worth, I'd really, really like to come visit you on winter break."

"Yes!" I cheered. "I'd like that, too."

"Good." He kind of laughed. "You better."

I marveled at his crooked smile one last time, forcing my brain to memorize this moment as I turned and walked to the door. As I neared the exit, I looked over my shoulder and called out, *"Less-than sign, number three."*

"Less-than sign, number three, you too," he called back.

☆ ☆ ☆ ☆ ☆

"So where's the plaque?" Belinda said the second I climbed the stairs to the bus.

"Oh!" My eyebrows shot up. In all the excitement of my musical-romance ending, I'd completely forgotten the excuse I'd made to chase down Teddy in the first place.

"I . . ." My eyes darted around the bus.

"Here it is, Jack!" Lou called, popping up from her seat. "It's right here on the floor. It must have fallen out of your bag when you sat down."

"Oh, *phew*," I said, loving my friend, perhaps more than ever. "Yeah, I'm glad I didn't lose it."

"Okay, okay." Belinda swatted. "Go take your seat. I want to be home in time for the *Wife Island* season finale."

I hustled back to my row, flashing Tanner and Lou a thankful grin as I ducked into my seat. As we merged onto the highway I looked at my reflection in the key-scratched glass, the golden Columbus skyline disappearing behind us like a fading memory. Thinking about the roller coaster of events we'd endured was almost too much to take in, so I decided to just relax and listen to the rumble of tires on pavement.

"Jack," Lou's voice whispered from across the aisle. "How'd it go? Is everything okay?"

"Everything's great," I whispered back. "Thanks for covering for me."

"Anytime, friend."

When I moved to Shaker Heights, I knew I'd have to adjust to life in a new city, but I never realized I'd also have to face all the stuff that comes with growing up. I'd taken on school bullies, overcome rejection, started new projects and said good-bye to others. I'd turned foes into friends and learned truths about myself, but what made them all seem a little less scary was knowing that I didn't have to face them alone. As the morning sun shined through the window, warm against my face, I thought of my friend across the aisle and the events that led us to this precise moment—Lou holding hands with the boy she liked and me, dizzy from my first kiss—both of us knowing that no matter what happened next, we'd have each other to lean on.

I think we were ready for our curtain call.

The Fantasticks

The Fantasticks is a classic American musical with music by Harvey Schmidt and book and lyrics by Tom Jones. The show premiered off-Broadway on May 3, 1960, and played 17,162 performances before closing on January 13, 2002. It is currently the longest-running musical in history. Though it never played on Broadway, both Tom Jones and Harvey Schmidt won the Tony Honors for Excellence in Theatre for their experimental tale of two fathers who plot to make their children fall in love.

Over the course of its nearly forty-two-year run, *The Fantasticks* became known for launching the careers of many talented young actors, particularly those cast as the couple, Matt and Luisa. Some notable alumni include Liza Minnelli, Jerry Orbach, Glenn Close, Santino Fontana, and Kristin Chenoweth. Due to popular demand, a revival of the musical opened off-Broadway on August 23, 2006, and continues to run today.

Acknowledgments

Jack & Louisa: Act 3 would not exist without the enduring support, love, and commitment of our amazing team at Penguin: Francesco Sedita, Sarah Fabiny, and Max Bisantz. Special thanks to Barbara White and Stacey Pannebecker of Gainesville Middle School in Virginia for sharing their real-life experiences in the world of theater competitions. To Kate's usual suspects—Jeff Croiter, Arnold and Chris Wetherhead—you all remain recipients of her immense gratitude and devotion. To Scott Bixby for being Andrew's extra set of eyes and real-life Teddy Waverly. To Ellen Bowen, Brent Wagner, and Nancy Carson for helping Andrew navigate the choppy waters of auditions, acting classes, and voice changes when he was a budding MTN; and to Leesa Guay Timpson, Rufus Patrick, and Doris O'Brien for providing Kate with enough inspiration and love from her days in the auditorium of Burlington High School to fill three books. Finally, thanks to the New York theater community, as well as the theater community at large, for reminding us on a daily basis why we do what we do.